SPLINTERLANDS

SPLINTERLANDS

John Feffer

Haymarket Books
Chicago, Illinois

Published in 2016 by
Haymarket Books
P.O. Box 180165
Chicago, IL 60618
773-583-7884
www.haymarketbooks.org
info@haymarketbooks.org

ISBN: 978-1-60846-724-2

Trade distribution:
In the US, Consortium Book Sales and Distribution, www.cbsd.com
In Canada, Publishers Group Canada, www.pgcbooks.ca
In the UK, Turnaround Publisher Services, www.turnaround-uk.com
All other countries, Publishers Group Worldwide, www.pgw.com

This book was published with the generous support of Lannan Foundation and Wallace Action Fund.

Cover photo taken at Huangyangchuan reservoir in Lanzhou, China, by China Daily/Reuters.

Printed in Canada by union labor.

Library of Congress Cataloging-in-Publication data is available.

10 9 8 7 6 5 4 3 2 1

CONTENTS

Introduction: Up on the Roof   1

Chapter 1: The Great Unraveling   11

Chapter 2: In Brussels   23

Chapter 3: In Ningxia   55

Chapter 4: In Gaborone   83

Chapter 5: In Arcadia   107

Chapter 6: In Extremis   135

Acknowledgements   151

For Karin, who makes things whole

INTRODUCTION

Up on the Roof

More than twenty-five years ago, as I sat on the roof of our house watching the neighborhood's furniture float down the street, I thought things couldn't get any worse. Everything I owned was under water. The capital of my country was ruined. Mother Earth was exacting its revenge upon its most arrogant inhabitants.

As it turned out, things got a lot worse.

If anyone should have anticipated the world's vertiginous descent into chaos, I was the most likely candidate. I was the author of *Splinterlands*, a bestselling book on the fracturing of the international community that made Julian West a household name (among the more discerning households at any rate) and launched an entirely new field.[1]

---

1 Julian West, *Splinterlands* (Dispatch Books, 2020). Hailed as a "masterful blend of explicit history and implicit futurology" by Adam Hochschild

That book also led the chattering classes to dub me, dismissively, Professor Chicken Little.

True, I'd been warning people that the sky was about to fall. I just didn't think it would fall on me.

No one predicted that the "extreme weather event" known as Hurricane Donald would flood Washington, DC, and its surroundings in 2022. I'd gone to sleep the night before expecting, at worst, high winds and heavy rains. I was roused from sleep by sirens and rapidly rising waters. My wife, fortunately, was on a business trip in Chicago. My children were safely abroad. It was dawn, and I'd woken to a nightmare.

From my second-floor window, I could see a river sweeping down our suburban street. My car had already disappeared beneath the roiling brown water. Behind me, I could hear something lapping against the stairs. The river, I soon discovered, had already claimed the first floor. I entertained the idea of diving in to retrieve my wallet and my computer, both of which I'd foolishly left downstairs. I quickly scotched that idea. They weren't salvageable, and I didn't have time.

There was no place to go but up. I grabbed my phone, put on two more layers of clothes, and climbed out onto

---

in the *Washington Post*, the book went into multiple printings, inspired a graphic novel, and was turned into a French "new new wave" film. It would also turn out to be West's only significant publication. (On a personal note, I first encountered the book as a college freshman: It changed my life.)

the roof. The chimney provided a small measure of shelter from the wind and water. From this precarious perch, I could see other families huddled on their roofs. We looked like a flotilla of refugees, our chimneys as masts in the storm. My neighbors held tightly to their most precious possessions: grandma's walker, a small safe, the family dog. Virtually all these things, including the dog, would eventually be left behind. There just wasn't room in the boats that finally came to get us.

"This is the end," a young woman kept repeating to no one in particular as we huddled in the fishing skiff commandeered by the Coast Guard. Rain lashing her face, she clutched her laptop to her chest as if it were a flotation device. "This is the end, and everything has gone to shit."

Just as those who don't live in the Arctic north lack a sophisticated vocabulary for describing snow, we hadn't yet found the words for the catastrophes about to befall us. For the time being, "shit" would have to do. Soon we would see the collapse of everything we considered so stable: the European Union, multiethnic China and Russia, and eventually the United States itself. We would be visited by an almost biblical succession of plagues: disease-bearing mosquitos, killer robots run amok, the perils of too much—and too little—water. Even our own genes turned against us, with multiple mutations that we unwittingly passed to future generations like defective holiday gifts.

I don't want to diminish the impact of Hurricane Donald. Several thousand people died. The economic toll ran into the hundreds of billions of dollars. The US capital moved to Kansas City.[2] But this was nothing compared to what came next. And still we haven't come to the end.

It would be easy enough to say that Hurricane Donald destroyed my family and so shift responsibility to acts of God. In truth, however, by the time Donald hit, our children had already run away—Aurora to Europe, Gordon to China, and Benjamin to somewhere in the Middle East. As for my wife, we reunited at Municipal Stadium in Hagerstown, Maryland, and spent a month with her brother in York, Pennsylvania. Our house had been destroyed; our neighborhood was a no-go zone. Just as the US government shifted its operations to Kansas City, I proposed we move the family home to safer ground, to Omaha, where I'd been offered a job at the University of Nebraska.

My wife didn't want to go to Nebraska. "We have a chance to start over," she told me softly. "You and me."

"That's what this is," I insisted. "The middle of the country. Far from the rising waters."

She just shook her head.

I thought our separation would be temporary. With no small degree of lobbying, I managed to arrange an appointment for her at the university's environmental studies department. But she turned it down and went her own

---

2 A proposal to return the capital to Washington after the trillion-dollar cleanup was narrowly defeated in Congress. A second proposal not to spend the money to rebuild Washington at all was defeated by an even smaller margin.

way. Aurora and Gordon never visited. I was all alone in my empty nest.

In the end, I didn't stay in Nebraska either. I'd been so focused on rising waters that I paid no attention to where water levels were falling. The Oglala Aquifer gave out a few years after I settled in Omaha, precipitating the Midwest Megadrought. Just like the Joads, I had to move on, along with so many others.[3]

Every time I moved thereafter, I seemed to bring less and less with me. Now I have practically nothing left, except my memories, and those are increasingly unreliable. Nor do I have anywhere else to go. All over the world, the waters are still rising, but I've stopped moving.

After all, I am old and living out my final days in an era that has no use for the elderly. My shrinking tribe comes from a vanished, prelapsarian world, so why should anyone listen to or care about us? We look backward when everyone else is facing forward. They are anticipating the next big thing. The only big thing that I'm looking forward to is death.

Long ago, tribal peoples gathered around the campfire in the evening to listen to the stories of their elders. The community drew strength and conviction from accounts of

---

3 The Joads, in the largely forgotten novel *The Grapes of Wrath* by John Steinbeck, moved from Oklahoma to California during the dust storms of the 1930s that accompanied the Great Depression. In 2026, despite some financial setbacks associated with the Great Panic, the author had hardly fallen to the level of a family of displaced tenant farmers.

where they came from and how they came to be. Parents passed such tales on to their children.

In what now may be the evening of our civilization, I also have a story to tell, even if there's no one around to hear it. I'm running out of time, so please excuse the brevity of my account. As I watch the embers of my campfire gradually lose their glow, I'm hurriedly trying to order my thoughts. I fear that it's a fool's errand. These days, we listen to our children, not they to us. Given what we've done to the planet, perhaps they have a point. Tasked with passing the baton, like hundreds of generations before us, my team has fumbled the handoff.

I look back not in anger but in regret. Given all that has happened to the world, my special regret might sound petty: my family has scattered to every point of the compass, and I'm not quite sure how this happened.[4] For many years, we lived together in some degree of harmony. My wife was engaged in work as urgent and as compelling as my own. We raised our three children according to our professed values.

Then, suddenly, it all broke apart, and I didn't see my wife or my children for years.

I suppose that many people, as they near their end, desire reconciliation. I don't believe in such things. Still, I do want to understand whether what happened to us was

---

4 West is being disingenuous here. He knew quite well why his family disintegrated. His concealing of this part of his story is a critical subtext to this report.

inevitable. Over the last few months, I've gotten back in touch with my family and learned, finally, what it was that drove us apart. I should have known earlier, but physicians can't operate on themselves, therapists can't cure their own neuroses, and intellectuals are blind to the very knowledge that can set them free. When they eventually come to this knowledge, it's usually too late.

Being a scholar, I've naturally clothed this personal quest in a larger project, having received a commission of sorts to write a report. This unexpected opportunity has led me to revisit the events of my life and its disintegration even as I revisit the themes of *Splinterlands*, my first book, the one I published so many decades ago on the fracturing of the international community.

When I was gathering the materials for my magnum opus, I had no idea that life would imitate scholarship. There I was, composing my precious manuscript in the comfort of my study, in the comfort of my household, in the comfort of my profession, little imagining that my little world would splinter just as surely as the larger world around me. I should have known better. In the great myths of antiquity—Oedipus, Antigone, Medea—strife only destroys the surrounding society after first tearing apart the family.

So, what you have in front of you is the result of a double quest. I returned to the archives to conduct a careful study of global developments over the last thirty years. I also made four site visits that just happened to coincide with the locations of my family members. The result is this report, which reexamines the question of why the Great Unraveling took place: in the world writ large, in my family writ small.

My travels are complete. I found what I was looking for. The answers, both surprising and painful, have in a way set me free. But as much as I would like to, I can't change the past. I can only describe it—incompletely, imperfectly—and hope that there will be a future not only for this manuscript but, my dear reader, for you as well.

Back in 2022, I sat on my roof and contemplated death for the first time. I had no confidence that the government or private charities would marshal the necessary resources in time to rescue my neighbors or me. I had already watched as three privateers rowed by offering their services at a price. I had no cash or credit cards on me, and they didn't accept promises of future payment. I don't remember any such stories during Hurricane Katrina in 2005 or even the Great Oregon Tsunami of 2019. But that's what was becoming of us: *homo homini lupus.*[5]

By the time the last of these mercenaries disappeared from view, the water had risen just above my gutters. My neighbors atop their three-story houses were miserable in the driving rain, but they could hold out longer. Those of us with two-story houses were beginning to eye the flotsam that drifted past as possible rafts of last resort.

---

5 "Man is wolf to man." West's favorite expression; it served as the epigraph to *Splinterlands.*

I heard the voice through the bullhorn before I saw the Coast Guard skiff. It sounded to me like the voice of God. The rain continued mercilessly, but for me that voice was the rainbow sign and that skiff the ark of salvation. I thought that the worst was over, that the darkness was lifting. How wrong I was.

I'd forgotten that even as God was offering hope with his rainbow and dove, he also made a veiled threat if mankind did not change its errant ways. "No more water," God promised Noah and the survivors. "But remember: the fire next time."

CHAPTER 1

The Great Unraveling

Water boils most fiercely just before it disappears. And so it is, evidently, with human affairs.

Before all hell broke loose in 1914, the world witnessed an unprecedented explosion of global trade at levels that would not be seen again for more than six decades. Before the Nazis took over in 1933, Germans in the Weimar Republic were enjoying an extraordinary blossoming of cultural and political liberalism. Before the Soviet Union imploded in 1991, Soviet scholars were proudly pointing to rising rates of intermarriage among the many nationalities of the federation as a sign of ever greater social cohesion.

And in 2018, just before the Great Unraveling, the world still seemed to be in a frenzy of what was then labeled "globalization." The volume of world trade was at an all-time high. Facebook had created a network of three billion active users. People on every continent were dancing to Drake, watching the World Cup final, and eating sushi. At the other end of the socioeconomic spectrum, more people were on the move as migrants and refugees than at any time since the end of World War II.

Borders, between countries and cultures, seemed to be crumbling everywhere. Once divided into a relatively stable mosaic of nation-states, the world was becoming liquid, a rainbow swirl.[1]

Before 2018, almost everyone believed that time's arrow pointed in the direction of greater integration. Some hoped (and others feared) that the world was converging on ever larger conglomerations of nations. The internationalists campaigned for a United Nations that had some actual political power. The free traders imagined a frictionless global market where identical superstores would sell the same products at all their global locations and happy consumers would sing the same jingles in the universal language of commerce. The technotopians prophesied a world united by Twitter and Instagram: a republic of social media. Of-

---

1 In *Splinterlands*, West famously introduced the concept of an "*ebru* world." In a critical passage, he wrote, "The Turks created a decorative style called *ebru*, a form of painting on water that produced a characteristic swirl of color. What had once been a clearly defined mosaic of nation-states has become a field of interpenetration." Although he is undoubtedly alluding to this passage in his mention of a "rainbow swirl," it's unclear why he makes no reference to *ebru*. Perhaps he grew irritated by the ways in which his metaphor has been misapplied over the years. See, e.g., the popular video-game app EbruWorld.

ficially, more and more countries were committing themselves to diversity, multiculturalism, and the cosmopolitan ideals of liberty, equality, and individualism. Pundits had already proclaimed the advent of a flat world, a borderless world, a McWorld.

In those years, people were so busy crossing borders—real and conceptual—that they barely registered the growing backlash.

Everything began to change in the mid-teens of this century, a phenomenon I first chronicled in *Splinterlands*. That book, it turned out, would be the foundational text for a new discipline that came to be called geo-paleontology. I shouldn't have been taken aback by my book's success. Everyone likes a good scary tale, even one dressed up in statistics and footnotes. And the best horror stories are never about zombies or vampires or bug-eyed aliens. They're always about the everyday terrors right in front of us. I was the first to point out what should have been obvious to anyone with a modicum of realism: the world was falling to pieces—and not in slow motion, either.

As a middle-aged scholar in 2020, I practically created geo-paleontology.[2] (We used to joke that we were

---

2 According to its WikiUniverse entry, geo-paleontology was founded not by Julian West in 2020 with the publication of *Splinterlands* but by the Korean scholar Chung-in Moon in 2019 with a series of articles on the collapse of the Sinocentric system. Rival Wikipedias alternately credit Dutch economist Jan Tinbergen, Albanian novelist Ismail Kadare, American sociologist Saskia Sassen, and/or Brazilian philosopher Roberto Unger.

the only historians with true 2020 hindsight). What we geo-paleontologists do is dig around in archives to exhume the extinct: all the empires and federations and territorial unions that have gone the way of the dinosaurs. We're interested in how the mighty are brought low. We look at the small fragments that remain and try to reconstruct what were once giants. During the twenties and thirties, when the modern-day giants were falling left and right, we were all the rage, less because of our acuity as historians and more because of our supposed prescience as prognosticators. As a result, we received a fair share of criticism for our supposed twist on Whig history.[3] But such controversies have long since become academic. Now that everyone is accustomed to the world as it is, they are less interested in how this world came to be. As a result, my profession is becoming as extinct as its subject matter.

Today, in 2050, ever fewer people can recall what it was like to live among those leviathans. In my youth, we imagined lumbering dinosaurs like Russia and China and the European Union enduring regardless of the global convulsions around them. Of course, at that time, our United States still functioned as its name suggests rather than as the current motley collection of regional fragments fighting over a diminishing resource base.

Empires, like adolescents, think they'll live forever. In

---

3 "West and his acolytes study the past with one eye on the future," wrote Jill Lepore in her otherwise favorable review of *Splinterlands* in the *New Yorker*.

geopolitics, as in biology, expiration dates are never visible. As a result, it can be hard to distinguish growing pains from death rattles. When the end comes, it's always a shock.

Consider the clash of the titans in World War I. Four enormous empires—the Ottoman, Austro-Hungarian, Russian, and German—went into that conflict imagining that victory would give them not just a new lease on life, but even more territory to call their own. And all four came crashing down. The war was horrific enough, but the aftershocks just kept piling up the bodies. The flu epidemic of 1918 and 1919 alone, which soldiers unwittingly transported from the trenches to their homelands, wiped out at least fifty million people worldwide. This, too, was globalization—of death. It would have been impossible to imagine such an outcome in 1913, when the silkworms of modernity—the telephone, the ocean liner—were spinning gossamer threads to enclose the world in a cozy cocoon.

When dinosaurs collapse, they crush all manner of smaller creatures beneath them. Who today remembers the final throes of the colonial empires in the mid-twentieth century with their staggering population transfers, fierce insurgencies, and endless proxy wars—even if the infant states that emerged from those bloody afterbirths gained a measure of independence?

My own specialty as a geo-paleontologist has been the post-1989 era, that distant period when surging hopes quickly gave way to grave disappointments. The breakup of the Soviet Union heralded the last phase of decolonization and the first hints of the new spirit of nationalism that would dominate our future. The redrawing of boundaries that took place in parts of Asia and Africa from the 1990s into the twenty-first century produced East Timor, Eritrea, South Sudan, and Somaliland, among other new states. The upheavals of the Middle East in the wake of the US invasion of Iraq and the "Arab Spring" followed a similar if far more chaotic and bloody pattern, as religious extremism tore apart the multiethnic countries of the region.

And yet, even in this inhospitable environment, the future still seemed to belong to the dinosaurs. Whatever the setbacks, the United States as the "sole superpower" continued to loom over the rest of the planet, with its military in constant intervention mode. China was on the rise, eager to absorb Taiwan, digest Tibet, and control the South China Sea. The Kremlin seemed bent on reconstituting some faded facsimile of the old Soviet Union, with Russia as *primus inter pares*. The need to compete on an increasingly interconnected planet pushed countries together to create economies of scale. The European Union deepened its integration and expanded its membership. Nations of very different backgrounds formed economic pacts, though who now remembers the North American Free Trade Agreement and its ilk? Even countries without shared borders created joint enterprises, like the Organization of Petroleum Exporting Countries and, later, the informal BRICS alliance of Brazil, Russia, India, China, and South Africa.

Indeed, after 1989, an odd ideological convergence seemed to be taking place. Gone was the bipolar world of communism versus capitalism. Yet, instead of seeing countries move toward a happy medium of democratic socialism, as some theorists of the 1960s had hypothesized would happen, the world headed toward a worst-of-both-worlds amalgam of market authoritarianism.[4] Even this, however, seemed to represent an integration of sorts, for the putative Communists in Beijing ultimately spoke the same language as the nominal Islamists in Ankara, the Euroskeptics in Paris and Budapest, and the America-firsters in Washington. They formed a kind of Nationalist International.

The leaders of these movements were not members of a single global party, nor did they even consider themselves part of a single movement.[5] Indeed, they were quite skeptical of anything that smacked of transnational cooperation. A Nationalist International, after all, is a contradiction in

---

4 West seems to be referring here to an essay from 2015, "Why the World Is Becoming the Un-Sweden," in which the author writes: "The convergence theorists imagined that the better aspects of capitalism and communism would emerge from the Darwinian competition of the Cold War and that the result would be a more adaptable and humane hybrid. It was a typically Panglossian error. Instead of the best of all possible worlds, the international community now faces an unholy trinity of authoritarian politics, cutthroat economics, and Big Brother surveillance."

5 In *Splinterlands*, West provided this short list of what he called the "prophets of disintegration"—Donald Trump in the United States, Recep Tayyip Erdoğan in Turkey, Hungarian prime minister Viktor Orbán, Russian president Vladimir Putin, French National Front Party leader Marine Le Pen, Indian prime minister Narendra Modi, Japanese prime minister Shinzō Abe, and Egyptian president Abdel Fattah el-Sisi.

terms. Yet, as a group, they heralded a change in world politics still working itself out thirty-five years later.

Ironically enough, at the time these figures were labeled "dinosaurs" because of their focus on imaginary golden ages of the past. But when history presses the rewind button, as it has for the last three decades, it can turn reactionaries into visionaries.

Few serious thinkers during the waning days of the Cold War imagined that, in the long run, nationalism would survive as anything more significant than flag and anthem. As historian Eric Hobsbawm concluded in 1990, that force was "no longer a major vector of historical development." Commerce and the voracious desire for wealth were sure to rub away national differences until all that remained would be a single global marketplace of putatively rational actors.[6] New technologies of travel and communication would unite strangers and dissolve the passions of particularism. The enormous bloodlettings that nations visited on one another in the nineteenth and twentieth centuries would surely convince all but the lunatic that appeals to motherland and fatherland had no place in a modern society.

As it turned out, however, commerce and its relentless push for comparative advantage merely rebranded nationalism as another marketable commodity. Travel and communication increased the opportunities for misunderstanding

---

6 "This was supposed to be the ultimate triumph of interests over passions," West wrote in *Splinterlands*, paraphrasing the economist Albert O. Hirschman.

and conflict. And a grey fog of amnesia obscured the knowledge that war is hell. Perennially underestimated, nationalism did not go gently into the night. Quite the opposite: it literally remapped the world we live in. This spirit of disintegration would, in the end, ensure that the bloodlands of the twentieth century would give way to the splinterlands of the twenty-first. The disunity that settled over our world came at precisely the wrong moment. As we are all learning the hard way, a planet divided against itself cannot stand.

The fracturing of the international community did not happen with one momentous crack. Rather, it proceeded like the calving of Arctic ice masses under the pressure of global warming, leaving behind only a herd of modest ice floes. Rising geopolitical temperatures had a similar effect on the world's map.

At first, it was difficult to understand how the war in Syria, the conflict in Ukraine, the simmering discontent in Xinjiang, the uprisings in Mali, the crisis of the Europe Union, and the upsurge in anti-immigrant sentiment throughout the postindustrial world were connected. But connected they were.

And connected to my family as well.

I have two sons, a daughter, and an ex-wife. Thanks to our latest technologies, I can communicate with them in the blink of an eye—indeed, *with* the blink of an eye. I'm rather old-fashioned, however, so I never opted for retinal implants. After all, the best technology in the world can't bridge distances that only one side wants bridged.

I began to reach out to my family two weeks ago. My daughter, in Brussels, responded almost immediately, and almost warmly. My older son ignored my messages, and only when I'd despaired of ever reaching him did he suddenly respond, apologetically, that a cyberstorm near his home base in Ningxia was responsible for his lack of communication. Did he really think I'd fall for that overused excuse?[7]

My younger son was the hardest to track down. Like me, he's kept on the move, and so I was forced to follow a trail of virtual breadcrumbs. In the end, to get his precise coordinates, I also had to rely on some outside assistance. The only emotion he expressed when we finally met was a begrudging respect that I, a relative Luddite, had managed to find him where so many had failed.

My ex-wife was easy to find. She's been living in the same place for the last twenty-five years. But she was perhaps the most reluctant to engage with me.

"What's the point of reopening old wounds?" she asked. "Aren't we too old for this?"

I couldn't think of a good response. So I said, "I want to leave an accurate record for our children."

"But that's exactly *why* I don't want to talk," she responded, with that little laugh of contempt that I loved so much when we were married and it was directed at others but came to despise so thoroughly when turned on me.

In the end, even she agreed to my proposal. Perhaps

---

7 Cyberstorms, in which weather events affect virtual communication, are a chronic problem in Ningxia. West's son was probably telling the truth.

my family was only acceding to an old man's wishes. I concealed the true state of my health—on the Internet, no one knows that you're sick as a dog—but perhaps they suspected that they would not have another opportunity for what we once called "closure."

Or perhaps they were touched that I actually wanted to see what their lives looked like. As it happened, my interest was not just personal, though I neglected to fill them in on my full agenda. My children's chief childhood complaint was the inordinate amount of time their parents devoted to their careers. My older son used to joke that *Splinterlands* was the fourth child in the family, and the only one that got any real attention. No doubt he would deride this sequel as a grandchild that has once again displaced him in my affections.

At first, my wife and children expressed surprise that I would even consider undertaking such long overseas trips.

"Oh, no," I explained. "I have no intention of flying or traveling on those nauseating high-speed trains."

And that's when I revealed my plan to spend a day with each of them virtually, thanks to the equipment I have here at this facility. They were surprised that I was willing to use such technology, even if it had long since become standard. Growing up, they used to ridicule me for relying on an actual calendar book to make appointments and for refusing to use an e-reader. That, of course, was in those pre-Donald days, before the hurricane washed away my calendar and destroyed my five-thousand-volume library.

The first stop on my trip around the world was Brussels, the place I was most looking forward to visiting—actually, revisiting. My daughter, my oldest, would guide me through the wreckage of what had once been the most prosperous, equitable, and welcoming region of our world. Until, quite suddenly, it wasn't.

CHAPTER 2

In Brussels

In 1990, when I was in my twenties, I spent an unforget-table summer in Brussels. I was single, unencumbered by children, and thrilled to be living overseas for the first time in my life. For a Ph.D. student in international relations, I had an embarrassingly pristine passport. As a young man, I'd been focused on getting through college and graduate school as quickly as possible to achieve my long-held dream of joining academia. Until then, I'd only had the time and money to do a bit of European travel as well as one appall-ing, never-to-be-repeated spring break in Jamaica.[1] Close to the end of graduate school, a fellowship afforded me the

---

1 West neglects to mention his first marriage to Alesha Kinbote, the result of this college trip. That long-distance marriage lasted less than a year. There was, however, a child—a son named Isaac—born shortly before the divorce became final. So, although "single" in Brussels, West was not technically childless.

chance to conduct research in Belgium, and I was determined to make the most of it.

Brussels, in those pre-division days, had a reputation as a boring, buttoned-down city, and I'd chosen a thesis topic very much in keeping with its rather prim focus on policy. But I made enough friends during my summer residency to sample some of the capital's more esoteric pleasures—a Congolese dance club, the best *waterzooi* hole in the city, a basement bar where you had to know the right knock to get in and sip cosmopolitans with the hipsters. I was young, and young people can find a way to party in even the most becalmed of cities.

My thesis research focused on what was then a controversial issue involving the European Union. Much of that summer I spent in the archives of the European Commission or conducting interviews in dreary offices trying to determine if the EU would expand its membership or bind its existing members closer together politically and economically.[2] The choice to "widen" or to "deepen" seemed vitally important at the time.

I had revisited Brussels a couple times after my daughter settled there, but not since the dissolution of Belgium,

---

2 In his first book, on the European question, West wrote, "The few people who predicted the end of the EU because it expanded too quickly or imposed too many requirements on its members were on the apocalyptic margins. The Berlin Wall was rubble and the Cold War was over. Everyone wanted to be European in those days." By the time West published his book in 1994, the wars in Yugoslavia were already raging. Even as a young academic, he was nostalgic for an earlier version of Europe.

which I observed sadly at a distance. I plugged into the city a few hours before my scheduled meetup with Aurora—just to refamiliarize myself with the tidy squares and Art Nouveau architecture.

I wasn't prepared for what I saw. My picture of Brussels was at least twenty years out of date. I expected a backwater, not a war zone.[3]

At first, it seemed that the city—at least the southern half that now served as the capital of Wallonia—had simply become run down. The apartment block where I'd stayed that summer sixty years ago was now abandoned, with families camped out in the wreckage of what had once been rooms. A formerly prosperous diamond district was now a haven for prostitutes, and its upscale stores had given way to cut-rate DNA outlets, seaweed discounters, and hovercar chop shops. There were still quarters that catered to the well-off, but even these could have done with a fresh coat of solar paint. Nor did I remember so much graffiti from my student days. On more than one wall, thanks to the imaginative hand of a guerrilla artist, the red rooster of Wallonia clawed

---

3 It's hard to imagine that West could have been quite so unaware of developments in the former Belgium. Later in the report, he writes that he did a month of research before embarking on his trip. Even if his daughter went to great lengths to conceal her deteriorating environment, surely he must have come across references to it in the specialized sources that we know he accessed at that time. It's possible that he is feigning ignorance here to heighten his account's dramatic effect, a technique that would raise the question: Where else did West alter the facts in order to tell a more compelling story? (See footnote 19 for an alternative explanation of West's "ignorance.")

out the eyes of the Flemish lion. I suspect that the lion had the better of it on walls to the north in Flanders. Even a couple decades after the split, the rivalry remained raw.

I'd always considered the Belgians, unlike the citizens of other multiethnic countries, relatively lucky. The divorce proceedings between the Flemish and the French-speaking Walloons were reasonably amicable, not unlike the way Czechs and Slovaks had negotiated the breakup of their hyphenated country so many decades earlier. Yet however amicable they may be, divorces still produce tragedies.[4] So it was with Belgium. Extended families found themselves divided by canton. Arguments broke out over the division of national treasures. And Brussels, so mixed up ethnically, experienced a few months of intensive and sometimes involuntary population transfers until a more or less homogenous North Brussels could be absorbed into the new state of Flanders and South Brussels into Wallonia.

In retrospect, I was lucky indeed during that first hour of my walking tour to remain within a relatively calm district. Here, in what the natives informally called the Zone Verte, people maintained a semblance of normality. In its prosperous core, the buildings were still intact, shops offered the usual tourist junk, and hovercars negotiated the invisible grid above our heads. At my level, pedestrians walked, talked, read, and ate with what seemed like manic energy. On the other hand, I wandered the streets at my leisure, a

---

4 West could, of course, speak from experience about the bleak side of divorce. His breakup with Alesha Kinbote was anything but amicable.

flaneur in the double-breasted pinstripe suit I'd chosen for the occasion. (In reality, of course, I was lying in bed in pajamas with a cup of hot tea on the table beside me).

I'd never been a fan of virtual travel, just as I've always preferred to read real books, not e-books or, even worse, texts that scroll directly across my retina. I like to be in bed with a warm body, not dabble in secondhand virtual sex. And, similarly, I want to immerse myself in the full experience of a place, not navigate a landscape of holograms, however "real" they might seem.

Still, given my brittleness, I didn't have a choice. It had been more than a month since I'd last covered any real ground. And so, even if I was only moving my eyes to traverse the streets of Brussels, it was still exhilarating, something like lucid dreaming. At times, I even fancied that I was short of breath from all the exertion.

As for my other senses, I would have liked to feel a Belgian chocolate melt in my mouth or sidle up to a bar to order my favorite lambic, just as I had sixty years ago. Of course, it would have cost a small fortune to buy one day's worth of the food and drink I enjoyed in 1990 instead of simulacra made of seaweed, and I don't have that kind of money any more. I could, of course, have arranged for a desktop printer to be set up next to my bed to produce an approximation of the real thing. But I was having a hard enough time just "strolling" in a straight line without bumping into anything. Walking while eating chocolate would have been quite beyond me. If I'd been a little more adept at the VR dropdown menus and the molecular misters in the face mask, I might at least have been able to reproduce the smells of Belgium that I've missed so much— the rain-soaked cobblestones, the buttery perfume of the cafés. I'd also taken a pass on the latest full-touch gloves. But thanks to the technology I had managed to master, I could at least see what had changed in the city and interact after a fashion with my daughter. As it was, sight and sound were enough to push an octogenarian like me perilously close to sensory overload.

For the younger generation, VR's navigational controls have become second nature. But I'd only experimented with the apparatus briefly some years ago at one of those academic conferences I once frequented. It was not like riding a bicycle. During the first part of my tour of Brussels, I was a walking hazard, colliding with walls and closed doors not to mention other avatars. At one point, I even got trapped in the back of a long-distance bus between two migrant workers, and couldn't figure out how to escape. As it turned out, the bus soon entered a VR dead zone, forcing an automatic reboot, and I suddenly found myself back at my starting point. Even the most fully VR-wired cities have such dead zones. As I got used to the apparatus, I realized that an indicator in the right-hand corner of my visual pane flashed red if I neared one of them and provided blink-sensitive GPS coordinates for avoiding it.

Not long after extricating myself from the bus fiasco, I acquired my "VR legs," as they say. Instead of gazing exclusively at the sidewalk or the corners of buildings, I became comfortable enough to take in the sights. Slowly I came to appreciate what the technology had to offer and, indeed, why VR was the kind of game-changer that the Internet had been for my generation.

But for every sight that stirred a pleasant memory of that long-gone youthful summer, I was confronted by something I wish I hadn't seen. The impact on the city's landscape of the disappearance of the European Union saddened me the most. The immense glass-sheathed edifice that once housed the European Commission presently serves as the headquarters for a private security firm. The Council of Europe's liaison office has been taken over by CRISPR International.[5] All that remained of the greatest geopolitical innovation in history—a fair and just riposte to empire and colonialism—was the cracked bust of its co-founder, Robert Schuman, in trash-strewn Cinquantenaire Park.

I paid my respects to this forgotten architect of European unity. Everywhere else, I was in a small crowd of grey avatars.[6] But here in Cinquantenaire Park, I was alone, and this made the experience all the sadder. With tears obscuring my vision, I must have wandered aimlessly for some time, because the next thing I knew I had inadvertently

---

5 This is West's first mention of CRISPR International. He neglects to point out that this outpost of CRISPR was not a corporate office but a diagnostic facility that took advantage of the low-wage workforce available in South Brussels.

6 West, in his ignorance of VR, must not have enabled the public display function. As a result, other avatars appear to him as grey outlines.

bumped up against the border of North Brussels. A red X flashed across my viewscreen, alerting me to the fact that I hadn't arranged for a V-pass to Flanders. I retraced my steps and the X vanished. The sight of those barricades running through what had once been a center of multiculturalism nearly undid me. I began to tremble violently in my bed and had to wait until the shaking subsided before I could move on.

And that's when I got into trouble. In my haste to get away from the hated border, I must have wandered outside the Zone Verte. Suddenly, I found myself in the midst of shock and awe.[7]

At first, I couldn't believe that the street battle was real and imagined that I'd inadvertently transported myself into a multiplayer 3D war game. But it soon became clear enough that the dead and the dying were all too real. The scene before me was a vision of hell, an updated Bosch painting. There were flames everywhere. As soon as a drone had extinguished a fire in one place, a laser strike or nanogrenade would start two more. Even if I didn't actually exist in that world, it was hard not to duck for cover during the combat taking place all around me. I had no idea whom the two sides were. I don't think it was Flemish versus Walloon, for I saw neither flag nor the dueling colors of red

---

7 West is referring here, rather loosely, to a US military doctrine of overwhelming force similar in some respects to the earlier German tactic of *blitzkrieg*. "Shock and awe," coined in 1996, was practiced most famously in the Second and Third Gulf Wars.

and yellow. The combatants were mostly young, and they certainly had sophisticated weaponry.[8]

I soon became aware of the gray outlines of the rest of the avatar audience. There must have been thirty or forty of us. Quite inadvertently, I'd become part of something I'd always despised: tragedy tourism. VR voyeurs like these went to the sites of wars, earthquakes, street riots, not to help but simply to gawk. It was evidently far more thrilling than the war movies of my youth, but it was also an age-old impulse: During the US Civil War, for instance, families would bring picnics to the bluffs overlooking battles. VR made the experience considerably safer. Some of my avatar companions were not content simply to watch from a distance. They waded into the gore. Both the spectacle and the spectators sickened me.

As I hurried away, I thought about the strong contrast between this part of Brussels and the Zone Verte. Not a single building was intact. The gutted remains of hovercars lay scattered in the streets. All pedestrians had fled. And now I saw, on my viewscreen, a warning that I must have overlooked in my confusion: I was in the Zone Rouge. Desperate to escape, I tried something new and "jumped" directly to the coordinates Aurora had supplied for our meeting.

I found myself outside a café. I could tell from the map on my viewscreen that only a few blocks separated it from

---

8 Based on the probable date of West's visit to South Brussels, the battle was likely a skirmish between the fan clubs of two football teams, Anderlecht and FC South Brussels.

the street battle I'd just witnessed, with the Charleroi Canal serving as a dividing line. Of course, this is a chief feature of the splinterlands. Just as an earthquake will collapse the penthouse and the basement together, so the geopolitical cataclysm of the last thirty-five years has fused the worlds of high and low. The only comparison I could think of from my own times was the Baghdad of the 2000s. The everyday violence that had once marked only the cities of the Global South now could be found at every latitude. Most cities had their Green Zones and their Red Zones.[9]

I took a few moments to compose myself before entering the café. I didn't want to show Aurora how upset I was.

Aurora is our firstborn. We named her after the sunrise, an indication of just how optimistic my wife and I were in 1998. Life seemed to stretch before us as a succession of potentially happy milestones. We couldn't stop ourselves from imagining her successes before she was even remotely capable of achieving them. Little Aurora was our hopes made flesh.

Perhaps this is where we acquire our notions of progress, from watching our children develop so rapidly from such frankly unpromising beginnings. Surely, if such a mewling lump can grow into a walking, talking, sentient being, then we high-functioning adults should be able to achieve so much more if we put our collective minds to it.

---

9 West overlooks similar, if somewhat milder and more informal, juxtapositions from his own era, like the proximity of violence and prosperity in his beloved Washington, DC.

Progress, at least in those distant days, was our default expectation. In its wisdom, nature has contrived that, barring untimely departures, we are not around to witness our children's mortality. Perhaps we are programmed to imagine only their endless advancement, and that of our societies as well. Until now, that is.

"You look good, Father," Aurora said when I sat down across from her at our café rendezvous. "You look very vital."

I didn't tell her that I'd chosen an earlier avatar that reflected none of my current wear and tear. I didn't want pity to cloud her perceptions, not when I needed her to be as honest as possible.

"You look very good as well," I lied. She had the same narrow, vulpine looks as her mother. Once, like her mother, she had been chic and sexy. Now, clothed in an uncharacteristically dowdy dress, she looked like a witch fresh out of spells. "How are your husband and children?"

"They're well. They'll join us for dinner in a couple hours."

I glanced around the café. It was made up to resemble something from old Brussels. I could tell from the prices, however, that the pastries behind the glass case and the drinks listed on an old-fashioned chalkboard were just seaweed simulacra. Still, patrons were paying a lot, even if only for the semblance of authenticity.

The café was mostly empty. Two Japanese tourists were poring over a hologram map. They'd failed to turn on their privacy settings, but I didn't know how to simultaneously engage the translation and eavesdropping functions in order to understand what they were saying. At a table near the entrance, a fashionably dressed young woman was waiting impatiently, tapping her foot and drinking cup after cup of the café's specialty: hot chocolate with a pouf of whipped cream on top. The only other patron was a bearded man at a nearby table, warming his hands on a mug of coffee. He had the build of an off-duty bouncer and was looking at us suspiciously.

"What about the . . . security situation?" I asked.

Aurora sighed. "I've resisted getting an escort."

"But?"

Her eyes flitted to the side, and the bearded man raised his mug in our direction.

"Meet my friend and colleague Omar," she said.

"Even here in the Zone Verte?"

She shrugged. "Because of the work I do, because of where I go to conduct interviews . . ." She didn't complete the sentence. "Omar also helps out when there's a glitch in the translation software."[10]

I knew from a quick infosearch that Aurora was still teaching sociology at Saint-Louis University. When she was younger, she had worked for the European Commission. It was what had drawn her to Brussels in the first place, back when it was the perfect place to raise a family.

"I took a detour through the Zone Rouge."

---

10 Omar Araabi was a third-generation Syrian living in Brussels. In 2053, during a trip to see a relative in the Zone Rouge, he was accidentally killed in a drone strike against a suspected Sleeper.

She grimaced. "I would not have recommended that."

"It was . . . ghastly. How can you live here?"

"You get used to it. How often did you go to Anacostia when we lived in DC? Or what about the Metro system? All the accidents, repairs, delays? That was the capital of the United States, and we had a Third World transportation system. We just adjusted our expectations downward."

"That was inconvenience. This is . . . inconceivable."

"We take precautions."

"And your children!"

"If we were rich, I suppose we could go off to an island somewhere, but we're not rich."

"Is it safe?"

"There's no such thing as safe anymore, Father."

After so many years in Brussels, Aurora spoke English with a French inflection, which lent a certain music to her sentences. It was hard to imagine that she was my child. She radiated cosmopolitanism, while I remained a typical unilingual American. Even as a teenager, she had railed against those she called "Yankee yahoos and North American know-nothings." In high school, she'd immersed herself in French and insisted on croissants and café au lait for breakfast. I'm not sure why she gravitated toward France. Perhaps it was simply to differentiate herself in the family.[11] In college, she studied Racine and wore a beret in an almost

---

11 In the memoir Aurora published in 2055, *A Child of the Splinterlands*, she credited a charismatic middle-school teacher with instilling in her a love of French culture and language.

deliberately comic affectation. She left for graduate work in France and never returned. Now she'd managed to turn herself into a European, but at a time when "European" meant something quite different.

My wife and I had been delighted that Aurora chose to become an academic. It was the future we'd imagined for her when, as a toddler, she'd shown a precocious ability to make fine distinctions. ("That is not a cookie, Daddy," four-year-old Aurora announced one night at the dinner table, "that is a *biscuit*.") When she became involved in the European Commission, during those last efforts to keep the EU together, I was thrilled that one of my children was involved in the greatest ideological fight of our generation, just as the Spanish Civil War or the Arab Spring had been for previous generations. Then Europe began to fall apart, and now even boring old Belgium had become a place where a bodyguard was as much a part of the extended family as a nanny and children played a grim schoolyard game called Red Zone/Green Zone.

"Old" Europe had practically disappeared. It can be found only in quiet farming villages in the Dordogne, mountain redoubts in the Tatras, and remote island hideaways like Aran and Nova Zembla, all of them now the province of indigenous pensioners and superrich interlopers. Old Europe, the Europe I loved and studied, was now just a nostalgic memory. Some elderly diehards, along with their more technologically sophisticated juniors, have even created a virtual European Union where they conduct what they call "political and economic business" as if the entity still existed.[12] But there is something beyond sad about that enterprise, like Civil War re-enactors or those Cold War buffs who once displayed their Lenin pins on black velvet pads.

In 2025, when I received the news that Aurora had taken a job at the European Commission, I had no idea that it would turn out to be such a short-term assignment. Alas, to pull apart even the most elaborate tapestry requires only a single loose thread. In the aftermath of the Arab Spring, the thread appeared in the form of a lifeline thrown across the Mediterranean. As a tenured professor teaching courses on European history, I watched how the chaos in the Middle East spread inexorably northward into my area of specialty. Iraq and Syria, multiethnic countries cobbled together by colonial powers, began to crack along ethnic and confessional lines. Under the pressure of a NATO air intervention led by the United States, Libya similarly fell apart when its autocratic leader was killed and its arsenals were pillaged and sent to terror groups across a broad crescent of crisis. The fracturing continued to spread—to Yemen, Egypt, Saudi Arabia, Lebanon, and Jordan. People poured out of those disintegrating countries like creatures fleeing a forest fire. The lucky ones headed for Europe, though in the end only a small portion were allowed to stay. The unlucky ones died where they were or during the perilous middle passage.

---

12 The project is still maintained at www.virtualeurope.com.

This vast flood of refugees by land and sea proved to be the tipping point for the European Union. Having expanded dramatically in the 2000s—the "wider" faction had won, as I predicted in the concluding chapter of my Ph.D. thesis—the twenty-eight-member association hit a wall of Euroskepticism, fiscal austerity, and xenophobia. Reacting to the rising tide of refugees, the anti-immigrant forces managed to end the Schengen system of open borders. Next to unravel was the European currency system when the highly indebted countries on the periphery of the eurozone reasserted their fiscal sovereignty. No more widening. No more deepening. Soon: no more Europe.

Once its soul had fled its collective body, Europe was but a corner of the Eurasian landmass, nothing more. Some countries, like Switzerland, remained reasonably prosperous, while others, like Italy, had slipped back into underdevelopment. In my youth, I read a memorable description of Rome in the Middle Ages: sparsely populated, disease-ridden, with wild animals scavenging among the ruins of the Coliseum.[13] How far it had slipped from the days of bread and circuses! The Renaissance rescued Italy and Garibaldi unified it, but by the middle of the twenty-first century it had again slipped into an almost medieval state of warring regions. In some places, the crime syndicates were the only organized segment of society left. I'd thought my daughter lucky to have chosen the relative safety of Brussels.

---

13 I have not been able to identify the source of this description.

And yet, after filling me in on Omar's unique talents and the security arrangements necessary to ferry my grandchildren back and forth to school, Aurora began lecturing me on just how wrong I was.

"Even visitors like you have to be careful," she was saying. "Identity theft. Avatar fleecing. Remember, Daddy, wide is the gate."

Even then I couldn't help laughing at her use of our family's code phrase for potential dangers lurking around the corner. "Wide is the gate and broad is the way" was, of course, a biblical reference, a passage that ends: "Beware of false prophets, which come to you in sheep's clothing, but inwardly they are ravening wolves."[14] We used the phrase whenever we were out as a family and we had to issue a subtle reminder that people at a nearby table were eavesdropping or the woman with a sob story was in fact a scammer.

"I doubt the ravening wolves would be interested in the likes of me," I replied.

"If you're not careful, a dozen phony Julian Wests will visit all of your banks and vacuum up everything you have. Did you buy avatar insurance?"

I shook my head. "They're welcome to what little I have

---

14 Matthew 7:15: "Because strait [is] the gate, and narrow [is] the way, which leadeth unto life, and few there be that find it. Beware of false prophets, which come to you in sheep's clothing, but inwardly they are ravening wolves. Ye shall know them by their fruits. Do men gather grapes of thorns, or figs of thistles? Even so every good tree bringeth forth good fruit; but a corrupt tree bringeth forth evil fruit."

left. And whom should I be worried about exactly? Anonymous? The Sleepers?"

"Right now it's mostly the White Tigers," Aurora said. "Kidnappings, assassinations, even illegal cloning. Anything to raise money to keep their operations going."

I knew about the White Tigers, of course, the infamous paramilitary wings of the various National Fronts across what was left of Europe. For the last decade, these right-wing extremists had been killing anyone suspected of being a Sleeper or pledging allegiance to the Caliphate.[15] In certain places, they'd even penetrated the police and whatever remained of national armies.[16]

"They're operating here in Brussels?"

"They're everywhere," Aurora replied. "First it was only the Lombards and the Basques. Now, every extremist wants a nanoautomatic for Christmas. When they're not assassinating Muslims, they're fighting each other. If it weren't so deadly, it would almost be funny. Just last week, members of the Flemish Tigers and the Walloon Tigers showed up at the

---

15 The "Caliphate," as West uses the term, applies to a number of different organizations that have expanded and contracted over the last four decades in what used to be called the Levant and in certain other outposts around the world. There has been a continuity of purpose to these organizations even in the absence of a continuity of structure and personnel. 16 The first White Tiger unit was established in Lombardy in 2030. Although previous paramilitary outfits had targeted immigrants—for instance the National Socialist Underground in Germany in the 2000s and the Soldiers of Odin in Finland in the 2010s—the White Tigers became Europe's first coordinated, continent-wide militia. By 2040, they had spread to every continent.

same house in Bruges to kill the imam of an underground mosque. They got into an argument over who should have the honor of making the hit. The conflict escalated, and they ended up killing each other. The imam escaped unscathed."

I was shaking my head.

"Come on, Daddy, get over it."

"I can't. This is not the Europe I remember."

"The Europe of cathedrals and art museums?" she said mockingly.

"The Europe of human rights. The Europe of tolerance and—"

"Please! Europe was heading in this direction even before I was born. You know that better than anyone. When I was a kid, instead of fairy tales at bedtime, you read me the headlines from the newspaper. The London Underground bombings. The neo-Nazis in Germany. I had terrible nightmares as a child."

"We tried to interest you in Harry Potter. You preferred the *Economist*."

"By the time I started working at the Commission in 2025, it was already far too late." She took a sip of her hot chocolate, then used her napkin to wipe a dab of whipped cream from her upper lip. "The National Front had won in France. The UK had pulled out. The EU was only a shell of what it once had been. We were the ones who shut off the lights and locked the doors. I don't think anyone really paid any attention to the Acts of Dis-Integration."[17]

---

17 By the time the Acts were finally signed in 2028, the EU had already

"But it didn't have to be that way, did it?" I asked plaintively.

"I'm sorry, Daddy, but that's just nonsense. And it had nothing to do with the immigrants coming from the Middle East or the anti-immigrant reaction. You were the one who taught me that the very idea of Europe was constructed in opposition to Islam. At the battle of Tours in 732. During the Crusades. Against the Turks and the Ottoman Empire. What we see now is more consistent with those roots. *Your* Europe—the Europe of multicultural unity—was an evolutionary detour."[18]

I brooded over her words because she was right, of course. She was just echoing everything I'd ever said to her. All my earlier anxiety surged through me again. During the twenties, after I'd published *Splinterlands*, I watched fretfully as the vision of the founders of the EU evaporated like so much steam.

We in America were committed to a lowest common denominator: the creative destruction of the market, the demagoguery of democracy, and the spectacular mediocrity of popular culture. But the EU had talked about "harmonizing up"—boosting its poorest members to the same level of prosperity as the richest. And it wasn't just words. Ireland, after it joined the EU in 1973, leapfrogged from

---

shrunk to a dysfunctional rump version of its former self.

18 Both West and his daughter were influenced by the work of Slovenian philosopher Tomaž Mastnak, particularly *Crusading Peace* (Berkeley: University of California Press, 2002).

an agricultural backwater to one of the wealthiest countries in Europe. European integration was a rebuttal to endemic inequality and the immiserating status quo.

Europe also represented the end of war. In the second half of the twentieth century, Europe overcame its internecine disputes, channeled armed conflict into political struggle, and gradually narrowed such political struggles down to polite disagreements over regulatory policy. That was to be the trajectory of mankind as well, from using our weapons to using our words.

That changed, of course, during those few decades on either side of the new millennium, the period we now call the Great Polarization. The middle dropped out of the world. Extremes of wealth and ideology flourished. Political moderates became an endangered species and "compromise" just another word for "appeasement." First came the disagreements over regulatory policy, then sharper political divides. Finally, as the world quick-marched itself back through history, came the return of the war of all against all. The EU, committed to the golden mean, had no way of surviving in such an environment without itself going to extremes. It was hard for me to give up on that earlier dream, because it had been, however briefly, such a viable and visible reality.[19]

"Things change," Aurora was saying. "And you just

---

19 This represents the most likely explanation for West's blindness regarding the deteriorating situation in the former Belgium. Because he simply didn't want it to be so, he pretended it wasn't—until he could no longer deny what was right before his eyes.

have to adapt."

I summoned up my favorite line from George Bernard Shaw, a playwright no one seems to remember any more: "The reasonable man adapts himself to the world; the unreasonable one persists in trying to adapt the world to himself. Therefore all progress depends on the unreasonable man."

"Today the mental hospitals are full of such unreasonable men," Aurora said, "Or they're fighting for the Caliphate."

"The Caliphate doesn't represent progress. It's a great leap backward."

Aurora looked impatient. "For you. For me. But millions of people are unwilling to adapt to what now passes for the modern world. The Caliphate, like your unreasonable man, is trying to adapt the world to itself. We just don't happen to agree with its principles."

We spoke of the Caliphate as if it were a single entity, but it was as fractured as the rest of the world. A Caliphate "affiliate" was born whenever two extremists with an Internet connection came together. Other than a would-be state with an unsteady income stream whose borders shifted constantly in the sands of the Levant, the Caliphate was little more than an archipelago of paramilitaries in the poorer countries and a decentralized network of Sleepers in the richer ones. But it did have a unified totalitarian vision that had become shorthand for an antimodern sensibility. Mind you, its members had no problem embracing the features of modernity they found useful—from VR and retinal implants to nanowarfare—even as they spoke of returning to the glories of the seventh century. From my perspective, it was the worst of all worlds. But it did allow the Caliphate's young acolytes, as one wag put it many years ago, to "have their sheikh and tweet it too."

"And you've been writing about the Sleepers?" I asked.

Aurora crossed her arms in evident annoyance. "No, Daddy. Third-generation French-Syrians living here in South Brussels."

"Are there no Sleepers among them?"

"There are Sleepers everywhere. Among the so-called natives as well. In terms of sheer numbers, the natives are responsible for more terrorism than the Sleepers."

I dredged up a memory. "Your latest publication is on identity politics, right? I saw one of your recent posts. What was it? On subaltern hybridity, yes?"[20]

She couldn't conceal her delight that I'd read something she'd written. She began talking with passion about her interviews, her quantitative assessments, new hybrid postcolonial identities that were emerging in both North and South Brussels. She was using a lot of academic terms I barely grasped. Perhaps it was a sign of age, but I found her research strangely beside the point.

"Daddy?"

I'd been trying to figure out the art projecting from the walls of the café. Or maybe it wasn't art. "Yes?"

"Why did you come here?"

---

20 Aurora West-Sackville, "Subaltern Hybridities in the Molenbeek Neighborhood," *Journal of Diaspora Studies*, July 2049.

"To see you. I hadn't seen you in a very long time."

"Why now?"

"I wanted to . . . find out why you hadn't been in touch."

"You know why."

I looked at her in confusion.

"I was so angry with you," she added.

"But why?"

"Do you really want to go over this again?"

I couldn't remember the specifics of our ancient argument, just the emotion, mostly hers. To conceal my confusion, I veered off topic.[21] "Are you still in touch with your mother?"

"We talk every week."

I suddenly felt an aching in my chest. "I'm so glad."

Aurora looked at me curiously. "She was here for the birth of Emil. And then Etienne. And you know how much she hates to travel these days."

I'd found out secondhand about the birth of my grandchildren. They were now in their early teens. I knew them only from pictures. I would see them later for the first time, along with Aurora's husband, a professor of medieval literature whose name had slipped my mind.

"What about Benjamin? I haven't been able to track him down."

"He's in Doha. As of last month."

---

21 It's possible that father and daughter did discuss the real cause of their estrangement, but that the conversation was too painful for West. He may simply have preferred to leave it out of his account.

"Do you have his contact information?"

She looked uncomfortable.

"It's not important," I said, hoping that this one data point would prove sufficient to find him. "But he's okay?"

"As okay as he'll ever be."

"I'm always scanning the newspaper, hoping I won't see his name."

"Me, too," she admitted.

"And Gordon?"

"We met in Paris two months ago. He often goes there for business."

"How's he doing?"

Aurora looked at me crossly. "Ask him yourself. Didn't you say you were going out to Ningxia to see him?"

"I value your opinion."

"As an informer? When we were growing up, it was like you were interrogating us in separate cells. What did you call your technique? Triangulation?"

"I was genuinely interested in what was going on in your lives."

"I thought that you were genuinely interested in controlling our lives."

"Gordon always complained that I didn't pay enough attention to your lives!"

"I love him dearly, but Gordon is a narcissist."

I decided not to go down that rabbit hole, so I switched topics again. "Then tell me what you think will happen here? In the future."

"Here Brussels?"

"Here Europe."

"The question doesn't make sense any longer. You know that."

"Humor me. Has the hemorrhaging stopped?"

"It's not a hemorrhage. That's the wrong metaphor. It's self-determination. People talk here of an Awakening. Three cheers for the Corsicans, I say. Three cheers for the Bavarians."

This made no sense to me. "How can you applaud when yet one more microstate establishes itself as a vehicle for the enrichment of a nationalist elite?"

"Some of the new states are quite progressive. Bretagne, for instance, has the most progressive constitution in the world."

"But where will it all stop?" I pressed. "When every neighborhood is a state? When every apartment building has its own flag and anthem?"

"You always warned me about *reductio ad absurdum* arguments."

"But everywhere I look, I see only tiny enclaves of green in a sea of red. That's what all of this nationalism has produced. A rising tide of blood. Even here in Europe."

"It was the direction the world was heading in. Why should Europe have been any different?"

"There used to be a common purpose. That's what Europe now lacks."

"The Bretons would disagree. They believe that they

have greater common purpose."

"But don't we desperately need a common purpose that unites more, not fewer, people?" I tried not to sound too professorial but probably failed.

She finished her hot cocoa. "Physicists now say that the universe is neither expanding nor contracting. It's oscillating. History, too, is full of oscillations. Perhaps your EU will return one day in a different form."

I'd heard that argument, couched in different terms, many times before. Empires rise and fall, then rise again under new auspices. The great city-states of the Greek Bronze Age collapsed in a series of conflagrations from 1200 to 1150 BCE, taking with them all of civilization's achievements in writing, art, and commerce. History repeated itself with the Romans, the Mayans, the Khmers. And each time, new growth emerged after the fires died down. "Having climbed to the top rung of the ladder of civilization," one of my favorite authors wrote many years ago, humanity took "a header into chaos, after which it would doubtless pick itself up, turn around, and begin to climb again. Repeated experiences of this sort in historic and prehistoric times possibly accounted for the puzzling bumps on the human cranium."[22]

I feared that this time around we were probably on our last "header into chaos." The entire planet was up against an existential limit. The fires "next time" had become the

---

22 The quote is from Edward Bellamy's *Looking Backward*, a book that we know influenced West in the writing of *Splinterlands*.

fires this time, and they were raging out of control with no firefighters in sight. And still the waters were rising, as all those displaced Miamians and Bangladeshis could well attest. I'd been mistaken: there had been no rainbow sign after all.

"We don't have the luxury of time," I said.

"Are you sure you're not confusing your own condition with the global one?"

I couldn't bring myself to speak of my fears to my own daughter. So I said, mildly, "It's hard for me to be hopeful at this point."

"Well, that's because you're—" She fluttered her hand.

"On the way out?"

"Stuck in your thinking. Every generation dreams of a golden age in the distant past."

"Maybe it wasn't a golden age." I indicated the body-guard with my eyes. "But it surely was better than the chaos that reigns in Europe today."

"Your expectations were too high."

"Me? You used to say that France was the only civilizing influence left in the world. And even your beautiful France has been drawn and quartered."

"I adapted," she said, simply. "And you haven't."

"Well, thank God you had a profession you could fall back on when the Commission folded."

She looked at me with sudden fury, and a feeling of déjà vu washed over me. "It was the worst mistake of my life!"

"To work at the Commission?"

"To become an academic."

"But you're so good at it!"

"I told you," she said, fists tight in her lap, looking like the sullen teenager she had once been. "I wanted to become a poet."

"You were good at that, too. But how many people make a living as a poet?"

She wasn't listening. "But no, you practically treated me like one of Pavlov's dogs. When I talked about poetry, you stopped paying attention. When I mentioned the possibility of graduate school, you gave me a treat. I learned to salivate at the very mention of a Ph.D."

"We attended your poetry recitals," I said, but in truth I couldn't remember one of them, or any of her poems for that matter.

"I became a professor because that's what you and Mother wanted—ever since I was a baby."

"But that's where your talents lay."

"Living up to your expectations," she said bitterly. "Even today when you said that you read my article, I couldn't help but feel so happy about it. Drool, drool."

"Aurora, don't you remember? It's what *you* wanted."

"I can't tell any longer where your expectations ended and my desires began. I went to work for your beloved Commission. I published in your beloved journals. I taught in your beloved classrooms. And it's all so boring I could scream!"

Omar looked in our direction with alarm. I gestured that everything was okay.

"But you could change. You're still young."

She was visibly on the verge of tears. "I am *not* young, Daddy. I'm fifty-two years old. I have a family. I have responsibilities. I can't just jump from one track to another. And even if I could become a poet now, even if someone walked up to me and offered me the position of poet laureate of South Brussels, if such a thing exists, I don't think I could write a single poem. Academia's jackboot presses down on my throat."

She could obviously still express herself poetically, if melodramatically. I've always been straightforward with my children. I never wanted to indulge their fantasies. Poetry is a lovely hobby, but Wallace Stevens worked in an insurance company and William Carlos Williams was a doctor. I remember telling Aurora all of this. Now I was beginning to remember that terrible, irrevocable quarrel we had nearly twenty years ago.[23] I understood suddenly that we were retracing our steps, but I had no idea how to . . .

A commotion broke out at a nearby table, the one where the young woman had been sitting and waiting. A man in a one-piece neoprene suit had arrived a few minutes earlier, placed his helmet on the table, and embraced her. I'd watched this reunion before being distracted by the argument brewing between Aurora and me.

---

23 West implies that his daughter's anger at being pressured to become an academic is the reason for their rupture. But, of course, we know that this was only a minor contributing factor. See Isabel Wilkerson, *The Wests: A Family Divided* (TMZ Books, 2043), 154–56.

Now, the couple was standing back to back in the middle of the café, brandishing plastic semiautomatic weapons. The guns looked like toys, but I knew that they weren't. To make sure that everyone understood, the woman fired a burst at the wall, turning one of the projecting artworks into a cloud of papery fragments. With their free arms, they seized the Japanese tourists and were now dragging them out of the café. The Japanese man was saying something in a mixture of French and Japanese, but I was too rattled to process the translation scrolling at the bottom of the viewscreen. The waiter had taken shelter behind the wooden bar. Omar had jumped to his feet, putting himself between Aurora and the abduction. He looked ready to pull out his own weapon.

"You should go," Aurora hissed at me. "Now!"

"But I want to make sure that—"

"Go!"

"Nothing can happen to me, but you—"Aurora rolled her eyes up in her head as if she were going to faint, then her gaze leveled out again and fell on my face.

"Go," she whispered. And blinked.

I was abruptly pulled out of Brussels and deposited, panting, back in bed, with a now-cold cup of tea by my side.

CHAPTER 3

In Ningxia

As soon as I caught my breath and my heart stopped pounding, I tried to contact Aurora. She did not respond. I scanned the news. There were no reports of kidnappings in South Brussels. I got in touch with the few people I knew in the area. No one had anything to add. I even donned the VR gear again and returned to the same café. Or I tried. A sign on the door indicated that it had closed early. Looking through the window, I saw overturned chairs and broken glass on the floor.

I walked around the block and found a police station, where a clearly overburdened staff ignored me. Avatars, I've been told, are only one step up from the homeless when it comes to the police. There are virtual law-enforcement agencies I could have contacted, if I'd known how.[1] Instead,

---

1 It would not have taken West much to figure out how to contact a virtual

I gave up and returned to my bed, exhausted though I'd barely moved a muscle below my neck.

I closed my eyes for a moment before continuing my search.

When I woke up, my pajamas were damp with sweat. The dressings on my feet had been changed. With some difficulty, I put on a fresh pair of pajamas lying on the seat of the chair close to the bed. When I glanced at the time, I was taken aback. My "nap" had lasted nearly twenty hours. The shades were drawn on my window, so until I checked the clock I didn't realize it was morning again.

I returned to the web to look for information about Aurora. Again there was nothing. I should have found this reassuring. Instead, I fretted. My family might have scattered to the winds, but it had survived hurricanes and droughts, wars and regime change. I was terrified that our luck was running out. For many decades after World War II, the industrialized world had been protected from large-scale violence and dislocation. No longer. Now I feared that the Great Unraveling had finally touched my family as well.

Even the loss of a single day could be fatal to my plan. I felt no pain in my feet but knew that the condition was spreading. I needed to keep to my schedule.

Although I'd slept more than planned, I still had an hour to prepare for my next meeting in Yinchuan City. My son Gordon had lived there, in the Ningxia region of Xinjiang,

---

law-enforcement agency, but the process would have been time-consuming, and he was already conscious of how little time he had left.

for more than twenty years. Indeed, he arrived when it was still part of China, before the Middle Uprising and the Four Evils tore the country apart.

This time I didn't get there early. I'd never been to Yinchuan before, and I was now all too conscious of my vulnerability as an avatar. I had no idea how Aurora had managed to unplug me from South Brussels, but I didn't want to wander around an unfamiliar city and expose myself to unknown risks. Perhaps someone had figured out how to take virtual hostages or administer neural shocks through the VR apparatus. I'd been briefed extensively on the safeguards and the problems of the system, and no one had mentioned these possibilities. Still, I was no longer willing to take any chances.

Gordon met me, as arranged, at the Drum Tower in the middle of Yinchuan. Only an hour earlier it had been dawn—at least for me—but here it was still the night before. A solid stone structure that straddled the intersection of two main roads, the Drum Tower was illuminated from below by a set of lights: yellow for the massive base, red for the pagodas that rested on the corners of its foundation, and a brilliant aquamarine for the shrine-like structure that rose out of its center.

Just as Aurora looked like her mother, Gordon looked like me. I've always found it unsettling to watch an entirely different personality animate such familiar features. He was tall and thin like me, but more athletic than I'd ever been, and with the same broad forehead, hooded eyes, and weak chin. He was not what anyone would call handsome, just as I had never scored high in that department. But he was confident, possessed of tremendous energy and focus. He was what people termed "magnetic." To solidify this impression, he grew a beard to hide his chin, let his hair grow over his forehead, and changed the color of his eyes to a brilliant blue. He was, I believe, on his third marriage. Aurora had hinted to me many years ago that he was a man of countless affairs. There were no offspring, at least none that I knew of.[2]

"Dad!" He greeted me with a big smile. "You look good."

I felt appalling, even after my deep and dreamless slumber, and I probably looked worse in reality. My mask of an avatar smiled back at him, and we set off on a brief walking tour of the city.

Gordon was eager to show me the sights. Embarrassingly enough, I'd never visited him before. A trip to Beijing fifteen years before was supposed to include an excursion to his adopted hometown of Yinchuan City, but the outbreak of the Middle Uprising had made all travel inland impossible, and another opportunity to visit that part of the world never presented itself.

---

2 In fact, Gordon had a daughter from an affair he'd conducted in his twenties with a Zimbabwean flight attendant. He had provided a monthly child-care stipend to the mother, and when his daughter reached eighteen, he invited her to visit him for several months in Ningxia. He made sure to spend at least one weekend a year with her in Paris, where she worked as an economist. Needless to say, his treatment of his illegitimate daughter contrasted sharply with his father's treatment of Isaac Kinbote.

I had no idea what Gordon did for a living, except that he worked in the field of "finance." Beyond that, his day-to-day activities were as mysterious to me as those of a particle physicist. He talked of "instruments," "margins," "drip algorithms." According to Aurora, he had made more money than he knew what to do with. Yet he continued to work long hours. He had no hobbies aside from forty-five minutes of squash three times a week. He apparently had no friends either: only lovers, former lovers, and former wives.

"Gulf money," Gordon was saying as he pointed to a pair of splinter-thin skyscrapers that bayonetted the night sky. "Sheiks. They like it here. These days, it's way too hot back in the Gulf, so the best families have set up here in Xinjiang. It's a majority Muslim country. There's plenty of desert."

"But it's so far from their roots."

"There's a historical link. The Ottoman ruler Nasruddin sent one of his sons here in the 1500s. He built the mosque at Najiahu, and all Chinese with the last name Na trace their ancestry back to Nasruddin and through him to the Prophet Mohammad's daughter Fatima."

"Apocryphal?"

"Doesn't matter. Of course, the Gulfies are also attracted by the economic opportunities."

"Like you."

"Yes, Dad, like me."

I really don't know where Gordon's interest in finance originated. Neither his mother nor I ever cared a whit about making money. We were comfortably middle class, of course, as a happy result of our work. But we didn't put in long hours to enhance our bank accounts. We were driven by other forces. Gordon was another matter. He learned how to program computers at the age of five. He designed his first successful phone app when he was seven.[3] He started his first Internet business at twelve and made his first million by thirteen. He graduated from high school at the age of sixteen, ignored our pleas to humor us by going to college, and instead started a "sovereign wealth fund," whatever that was. Like many of his generation, he followed the scent of money to China, spending a few years learning the ropes and the language in Shanghai before setting off for Ningxia, where, as he put it cryptically, the "margins are mouth-watering."

"You haven't heard from Aurora, have you?" I asked.

"No, why?"

I described what had happened at the end of my visit to South Brussels.

Gordon shrugged. "She's a big girl. She knows her way around."

"Aren't you at all worried?"

"If it had been a kidnapping, I would have been the first to know. They always locate the person who stands to lose the most."

---

3 West errs here. The first iPhone apps were introduced in 2008, when Gordon was eight years old. It was the following year that Gordon introduced his iAbacus app. He was precocious, but not quite as precocious as West makes him out to be.

"Money."

"Yes, money."[4]

"Can you make some enquiries?" I had no idea what this might entail, but I assumed that someone with as much wealth as Gordon commanded would have a commensurate amount of power, not to mention the connections that doing business in the greater Chinese region required.

"Of course. But I wouldn't worry. If you didn't see any news alerts, I'm sure she's fine. Tell me, did you two have an argument?"

"Well, I suppose you could say that."

"That's it, then. She's mad at you, Dad. Or perhaps I should say: *still* mad at you. She'll get in touch when she feels like it. But don't worry. I'll see what I can find out."

"And Benjamin?"

"I assume you want to see him, too."

"If I can find him."

"So you can argue with him as well?"

"Aurora said he was in Doha."

"Not any more. He's now in Africa. Botswana."

"What's he doing there?"

"That's . . . proprietary information."

"If I can track him down, I guess I'll find out. Has he ever been out here to visit?"

---

4 It's striking that West and his son don't talk about Isaac Kinbote here, since his case was all too relevant to their discussion. Of course, it's possible that they did, and that West was again selective in what he wrote down. To be fair, it's also possible that illness impaired West's memory.

"Benjamin?" Gordon laughed. "No, little brother has never had any reason to come out here. Look around. It's too stable."

The streets of Yinchuan City were clean, the storefronts full of merchandise. Young women, some wearing headscarves and others not, were walking in pairs but also unaccompanied. It was nighttime, and these solitary strollers didn't seem at all nervous.

"There are lots of mosques," I observed.

"The place is thick with mosques," Gordon said. "Mosques and banks. Thank God for the banks. Otherwise I'd find this a very boring place. If it weren't for the influx of Gulf resources, Xinjiang would have suffered the same collapse as China. But economic stats here over the last fifteen years are nothing short of miraculous."

I'd seen a lot of prosperous-looking people on the streets. But I'd also seen a scattering of beggars. I pointed out to Gordon the nearest one, an armless young man. With his toes, he grasped a small card, waving it at passersby to get their attention. The card had a QR code on it, presumably linked to his credit account. A passing woman didn't even glance at him, simply bent slightly at the waist to wave her palm across the QR code, making what was probably a small donation.

Gordon avoided the young man's dirt-encrusted foot. "Yes, it's part of the culture. Look, the growth rate here has been astounding. Not long ago, there was one ten-year stretch of double-digit growth, year after year. The per capita GDP puts Xinjiang in the top twenty. But the GINI coefficient—not so good. The usual extremes of rich and poor. No unions. Favorable tax rates for corporations. Very little in the way of a regulatory regime."[5]

"Your kind of place."

Gordon shrugged. "It has regulations when it counts. I've never been in such a safe environment. No alcohol. No guns. No organized crime. Paris is a war zone in comparison. And forget about Brussels. Poor Aurora."

"Sleepers?"

"There have been a few, but they've been stoned to death. Oh, don't look so aghast. It's a very effective deterrent. And it's a punishment reserved for Sleepers. Otherwise, it's quite a progressive place. The veil is optional. The president some years back was a woman, and several years ago an openly gay man became the mayor of Yinchuan. There are lots of BXs—"

"BXs?"

"Sorry—it's the slang term we use for transgender people. Comes from *bian xing*.[6] This isn't exactly the crazy country of Northern California, but there's a huge creative class and I've never encountered any restrictions. There's a store on the outskirts of town that sells whiskey to us

---

5 Xinjiang was well known then as the Switzerland of Asia: a parking lot for offshore capital. Gordon West made a considerable amount of money managing such funds and advising the state on how to ensure that the capital would keep flowing.

6 *Bian xing* literally means "sex change" in Mandarin.

expats. And even *I* don't need any bodyguards. You met Omar, I imagine. He wouldn't have much work here."[7]

I looked around. It hadn't even occurred to me that Gordon was unaccompanied. Such a rich man, yet he felt no need for protection. Admittedly, he had never been ostentatious. Even now the only sign of his wealth was his gold wedding ring. In his open-collared shirt and casual sports jacket, he could have been a tourist showing his avatar friend a night on the town.

"Not even your wife?" I asked.

Gordon laughed. "She's the daughter of a high Party official. People wouldn't dare threaten her with bodily harm. They won't take the risk of criticizing her behind her back."

I wasn't sure what Party he was referring to since I wasn't up on local politics.[8]

"You'll meet her in an hour at the restaurant. You still

---

7 Gordon exaggerates the liberality of Xinjiang. The woman president to which he refers, Na Jiabao, served only the remaining year of her deceased husband's term. The mayor of Yinchuan he describes as openly gay declared his sexuality only *after* his term was over. And although the crime rate was low in comparison with the neighboring remnants of China, there was no way to fully protect Ningxia from the turmoil in those lands. Gordon glosses over the fact that the province was experiencing a half-dozen terrorist attacks a year, and the government in Ürümqi was spending billions of yuan on drone strikes inside the country and along its borders. Since Gordon was a consultant to the Ürümqi government, it's hardly surprising that he presents the rosiest picture possible of his adopted homeland.

8 The ruling party, to which Gordon was no doubt referring, at that time went by the name of the Xinjiang National Liberal Party. Every few years it changed its name to provide a semblance of democracy.

like spicy food, right? I hope you have a good printer. The older models just don't do justice to authentic Xinjiang cuisine. It comes out tasting like bad American take-out."

I didn't have the heart to tell him that I didn't have any printer at all. I'd have to appreciate the meal with my eyes alone.

"Mei-hwa is eager to meet you," he said. "She doesn't speak English, but you received the Mandarin plug-in I sent you, yes? Much better than the default translator that comes with the standard VR package."

"I'm sorry I couldn't get out here for the wedding."

"You didn't miss anything. No booze and too many speeches. But it's all good. She's an amazing woman, Dad. I am a very lucky man."

Gordon had always been lucky, and not only in his investments. He'd relocated to China before the global economic slowdown of the 2020s undermined the implicit social contract the Chinese Communist Party had developed in the wake of the Tiananmen Square protests of 1989: incremental improvements in prosperity in exchange for political quiescence. From double-digit growth, the economy descended to single digits and then utter stagnation, after which the country began to come apart. Beijing's crackdown on anything that smacked of "terrorism" only pushed the Uighurs of Xinjiang into open revolt. The Tibetans, too, continued to advance their claims for greater autonomy. Inner Mongolia, with almost twice as many ethnic Mongolians as Mongolia itself, similarly pulled at the stitches that held the country together. Taiwan stopped talking about cross-Straits reunification; Hong Kong reasserted its earlier status as an *entrepôt* outlier.

But such rebellions on the peripheries paled in comparison to the Middle Uprising of 2029. In retrospect, it was obvious that the underemployed workers and farmers in China's heartland, who had only marginally benefited from the country's great capitalist leap forward of the late twentieth century, would attack the political order. But who would have thought that the Middle Kingdom could so quickly lose its middle? The smart Communist Party officials who saw the writing on the wall—quite literally, since the first signs of discontent were the "big character" posters denouncing the government that went up at the universities—aligned themselves with the new nationalist movements, including the Great Han Renewal Party. The waverers, not to mention the diehard party loyalists, disappeared into the vortex.

Out of this turmoil—secession at the edges and revolution at the center—the new country of Xinjiang had emerged as the most viable of the successor states. The provinces of Gansu and Ningxia had eventually attached themselves to this vast landlocked country, and Gordon had eventually attached himself to rising Ningxia. If he'd stayed in Shanghai, or worse, gone to Beijing, he might have lost his fortune or even his head. The Four Evils—extreme weather, hunger, splittism, war—had claimed millions of lives.[9]

---

9 "Splittism" is the common translation of *fen lie zhuyi*, the phrase the Chinese Communist Party once used to describe secession.

"I imagine that you'll find this unappetizing," Gordon was saying, as we entered a courtyard ringed by a colonnade and dominated by a tall octagonal tower made of beige bricks, "but there is money in chaos."

"Hasn't that always been the case?"

"Yes, but I systemized the process. Not to boast, but those early currency speculators who bet on a drop in the value of British sterling were pikers. I was the first to come up with a financial model of climate change. Then I applied that model to nationalist uprisings."[10]

"You're saying that you made millions off other people's suffering."

"Millions?" Gordon looked at me sternly. "I was a millionaire before I was fourteen."

"When you were still accumulating money the old-fashioned way: by making things, not destroying them."

"Welcome to the modern world, Dad. The United States became a wealthy country because of World War II. Japan profited hugely from the Korean War. And South Korea made it big because of the Vietnam War. There's always been enormous profits in large-scale suffering."

"So why are you telling me this?"

"You know how much I like to needle you."

---

10 For a dissection of Gordon West's contributions to the field of disaster economics, see, for instance, Paul Krugman's invaluable last book, *Gordon West: Pioneer of Chaos* (Princeton-Butler University Press, 2037). It's odd that neither father nor son mentions the book here. Gordon was reportedly unhappy with some of Krugman's criticisms. His father, out of envy, may simply not have read the book.

"I'd hoped you had outgrown that. Aren't you also going to tell me that you're using all this money to improve the world through your designated charities?"

"No," Gordon said. "I don't believe in charity. I give away the absolute minimum here in Ningxia to keep up appearances. One of the mosques on the outskirts of town is mine."

I was astonished. "You converted?"

"To what?" He laughed. "Pragmatism? Charity is one of the five pillars, and it's good for business to be perceived as devout. I also give to the State Opera, but I've never set foot in the place. Dreadful caterwauling."

"So, if you've not become a great benefactor, what are you using all your money for?"

"To make more money."

"But to what end?"

"Dad, that's the wrong question. There is no end. There is only the Way."

"You've found the Way? I doubt the original Taoists had finance capitalism in mind."

Gordon flashed his trademark smirk. "No, they didn't. They were obsessed with harmony. And I make money precisely where the system moves out of sync. That's where the opportunities lie. Not in the middle, but at the margins. *There's no money in the middle.* I patented that phrase, by the way—and made a lot of money out of it."

Gordon was right: there was no longer any money in the middle. The promise of a stable job and income—the iron rice bowl in the East and the ironclad pension in the West—had disappeared into a maelstrom of inequality. The superrich had effectively seceded from society while not only the poorest of the poor but many others plunged through a safety net as porous as cheesecloth. Pundits once promoted the "sharing economy" of millions of employees turned entrepreneurs. They applauded the "long tail" of a splintering consumer market: The mass market is dead, long live the niche market! Or so the boosterism of the moment went. In reality, a reserve army of the entrepreneurial now ran what was left of the service economy, just getting by on their sixteen-hour days. The poor sold their blood, their organs, their DNA, their avatars, anything to scrape by. The bottom line was grimly straightforward: The forces that could have acted to countervail the competition of the market and the ravages of climate change gradually disappeared. Gone was the guiding hand of the government. Gone were the restraining pressures of morality. It was everyone for themselves. To each according to his or her avarice, from each according to his or her naiveté. The sharing economy, it turned out, was the uncaring economy.

The application of market principles to every facet of existence had whittled away the public sphere in favor of the private realm until there was practically no public left. Consider, for instance, the disintegration of the US public school system, an institution that had shaped national identity during the formative years of generation after generation. Replacing it was a patchwork of high-performing magnets, low-performing charters, a dizzying variety of homeschool curricula of varying quality, and for so many children, of course, nothing at all, except the scramble to exist.[11] When a national educational system disappears, the nation itself is sure to follow, as it did in North America. Reproduce that development in hundreds of countries and the international community didn't have a chance.

Technology certainly played a role in this transformation, as computers and cell phones untethered individuals from fixed workplaces and then biochips turned each individual into his or her own work station. With the growth of VR came the rise of the avatar economy, in which the enterprising few could participate in a half-dozen jobs simultaneously without moving from their living-room couches. Everything became precarious, everything short-term, as each job's obsolescence was keyed to the technology that supported it. As one popular tweet put it: "Goodbye #socialsecurity, hello individual insecurity :("

The true midwives of this transformation were financiers like my son Gordon. The breakdown of the post–Bretton Woods system—of international financial institutions, flexible exchange rates, and the dollar as the global reserve currency—had been a boon to the financial class and, at first, to transnational corporations as well. The proliferation of tax havens, facilitated by these financiers, made it impossible for national governments to raise

---

11 Interestingly, West sent all three of his children to private schools in Washington, DC.

enough revenue to provide effective social services. Soon enough, voters came to associate the national state with sticks rather than carrots—or "sticks for us and carrots for them," where "them" included the unemployed, minorities, immigrants, and other vulnerable groups. Adopting a fashionable "antipolitical" stance, the masses withdrew their support for the state.

I confess that I never really understood the economics of this transformation, though. I studied the mechanics of currency controls and wrote about the rise and fall of Treasury bonds, panda bonds, and even bear market "Barry" bonds. Still, how the cosmopolitan club of bankers and financial analysts not only managed to find a berth in this new system but helped create it in the first place with their investment decisions always eluded me.[12]

"And you don't feel any scruples about hastening the end of the middle class?" I asked my son.

"Why should I regret the end of the vast mediocrity spawned by the Industrial Revolution?"

"You're ignoring the prosperity and security enjoyed by hundreds of millions of people."

Gordon dropped his façade of jocularity. "It was illusory, Father. Who ate up the resources of the world? You and mother, and the hundreds of millions like you who drove cars and ate hamburgers and went on expensive cruises."

---

12 Indeed, one of the major criticisms of *Splinterlands* was its superficial analysis of the financial determinants of regime collapse. See, for example, Nassim Nicholas Taleb's review of the book in the *Economist*.

"We shared one car. We avoided red meat. We never went on cruises."[13]

But my son was just shaking his head. "As if that really matters. A locust on a diet is still a locust."

As we were talking, Gordon had led me into the tower at the center of the courtyard. A tight spiral of steps brought us high above the city. From the round windows on the top floor, I looked down at the verdant courtyard that we'd been circling. Gordon, though, directed my attention beyond it.

"Do you see how far Yinchuan City stretches? The insignificant capital of an insignificant province of a once vast country. When I moved here, the population was two and a half million people and growing. And it didn't even crack the top hundred Chinese cities. Nibble, nibble, nibble: eating up all the food and sucking up all the groundwater. The desert was closing in on all sides and the scientists were desperately trying to keep the sand at bay. All part of China's expanding middle class. It couldn't continue like that."

"And it didn't."

"Do you remember what Americans were saying at the time?" Gordon adopted a ludicrous Midwestern accent: "'And what will happen when all those Chinese have cars? And what will happen when all those Indians discover how

---

13 West manages to omit any mention of the cruise he and his wife took to Nova Scotia in 2021. Given the role that the cruise played in the break-up of this family, it's perhaps not surprising that he avoids it here. West undoubtedly wished that he had never gone on that trip in the first place.

tasty bacon is?' There's nothing like the collapse of the global economy to recalibrate everyone's expectations."

"And your solution was for only rich people to enjoy such things?" I barely stopped myself from saying "rich people like you."

"It wasn't my solution. The market simply corrected itself. We were riding the tiger. And then we fell off, and the tiger did what tigers do. It ate us."

If we'd all been living in error, as Gordon suggested, then the market had indeed "corrected" itself. The great financial meltdown of 2023 had wiped out the savings of the middle class globally—the pension funds, the money market accounts—and effectively destroyed the international financial system. Gordon, from his new perch in Yinchuan, had bet on economic collapse, and he won big. Virtually everyone else had lost.

And so many of the predictions I had made in my book *Splinterlands*, published three years earlier, then came true. The financial meltdown had been like a huge comet crashing into the earth. The dinosaurs of that moment were not nimble enough to survive. The EU exited the stage. China began to unravel.

Shortly after the financial comet hit, I was in Moscow on a fellowship to study the reasons for the collapse of the Soviet Union back in the 1990s. Instead, I had a front-row seat as Russia collapsed in a spectacular fashion. I barely made it out before the third and last Chechen War began. For several years, the entire territory became a no-go zone.

The Russian unraveling began when the country's last Soviet-era politicians attempted to reconstruct the old federation through new Eurasian arrangements while at the same time trying to expand their jurisdiction over Russian-speaking populations through "frozen conflicts" with Ukraine, Georgia, and Moldova. A very twentieth-century thing to do, it collided with twenty-first-century sensibilities.

In its grab for more, the Kremlin was left with less. Mother Russia could no longer corral its children, neither the Buryats of the trans-Baikal region nor the Sakha of Siberia, neither the inhabitants of westernmost Kaliningrad nor those of the maritime regions of Primorye in the far east. In addition, a decade earlier Moscow's entrance into the Syrian conflict had contributed to an upsurge in separatist sentiment in the trans-Caucasus republics of Chechnya and Dagestan. The economic crisis delivered the fatal blow, for Moscow could no longer provide anything worth having to its far-flung regions. The collapse of energy prices robbed the Kremlin of leverage. Severing ties with the former imperial center became a perfectly rational economic decision. In the Second Great Perestroika of 2025, Russia finally divided along the lines we know so well today, separating into its European and Asian halves, into its industrial wastelands in the north and its creeping deserts in the south.

"Embrace the change," Gordon was saying, as he led the way back down the spiral staircase.

"Did you patent that phrase too?"

He laughed and gestured at the brick wall, which I longed to reach out and touch. "This is the Chengtian Temple Pagoda. It was built in . . ." He paused and I saw his eyes narrow and dart to the side in a retinal scan for information. ". . . 1050 in the Song Dynasty. An earthquake in 1738 nearly destroyed it. But it was rebuilt in 1820. Many other structures were destroyed in that earthquake, and they were not rebuilt. We have a choice. We can mourn the things that no longer exist and we can't even name, or we can celebrate what remains standing and try to make it stronger."

"But what if the destruction of the market is not creative? What if it's uncreative?"

"You might as well complain about evolution. I'm sure we could have done a lot of interesting things with a tail. And maybe, thanks to CRISPR International, some of us will have tails again in the future. But really, it's not for us to say whether something is creative or uncreative."

"Humans didn't create evolution; evolution created us. But we created markets."

"Which we controlled when they were located in the village square. But after markets achieved a certain level of complexity, they assumed a life of their own."

"Like the broom and the sorcerer's apprentice. And we know how that turned out."

"You're blaming the broom, Father, rather than the apprentice."

"We're all apprentices," I observed. "And that's the problem. The broom has practically swept us out of the room."

"The market is not the problem. If we had maintained our Protestant work ethic, we wouldn't be in the current crisis. It's the other killer apps that—"

"Killer apps?"

"You know, the other killer apps that helped the West pull away from the rest—science, medicine, property rights, competition, and consumerism—these were the building blocks of the Industrial Revolution. We didn't realize that these apps would ultimately kill us."[14]

"I'm not following your logic."

I didn't like the look in my son's eyes. He started to speak more slowly. "Until 1800, this right here, China, was the center of the global economy, of trade, of industry. And because of these killer apps, the West suddenly took off. They were the basis for the Western middle class that you loved so much. But they were like fast food. They gave the West a short burst of energy but were useless when it came to the marathon slog of economic development. The fat clogged up the arteries, and the sugar destroyed the metabolism. That was consumerism. We ate and ate until we were obese and the world couldn't support our weight anymore."

"If you have such clarity about what went wrong," I said impatiently, "I don't understand why you decided to profit from these trends instead of helping fix them."

"I'm here in Xinjiang, aren't I? It's a world-class managed democracy, and I'm one of its managers."

---

14 Gordon is making a somewhat obscure reference to a book published in 2011 called *Civilization* that enjoyed a brief moment of notoriety.

"Helping to prop up a democratic dictatorship?"[15]

"I've put my money to good use here," Gordon replied stiffly, "helping maintain order in a chaotic world. And you? What did you do with the money you made from your book? From your lecture fees?"

"It was hardly a lot of money."[16]

"Money is money. You can pretend something else, but basically we've done the same thing. The only difference is the scale—and that I'm not a hypocrite."

"That's ridiculous!" I protested.

This was, of course, a version of the argument we'd been having for years, for decades, but never before had Gordon come out and directly accused me of hypocrisy. I was surprised. He rarely made reference to moral failings. For years his epithet of choice was "behind the curve." Hypocrisy, if it provided a market edge, was perfectly justified.

My wife and I had always been concerned about what we felt was Gordon's lack of a moral center. At first, we thought he had some form of Asperger's, given his preference for numbers over people. But he ultimately had no problem communicating or picking up on social cues. For years I harbored a suspicion, which I didn't share with my wife,

---

15 Xinjiang emerged as one of the first "democratic dictatorships" of the 2030s: countries with the trappings of democracy, including free elections, but in which ruling parties stage-managed everything in the interests of "preserving stability" and, of course, their own power.

16 Although West didn't make anything near what his son earned, he did receive considerable royalties from *Splinterlands* and commanded five-figure lecture fees until the time of the Great Panic.

that he might simply be a sociopath, given what seemed to be his total absence of conscience. When I became more familiar with the circles in which he was traveling, I realized that my son was closer to the norm than I cared to admit. Based on their behavior, an entire well-functioning class of people—the leaders of business, financial institutions, political parties—deserved that label, for they cared not a whit about the well-being of society. Their professed concern for "social order" was simply a preference for a stable environment that would help them pursue power or money.

"We all tell ourselves fairy tales before we go to bed at night," Gordon said. "You've told yourself the same one for years, and it's helped you sleep. Far be it from me to insist that you start telling yourself a different fairy tale."

I had no desire to continue the argument. "So," I said, "if you have all the answers, what does the future look like?"

"The future of what?"

"The world."

"I don't make bets on the future of the world any more. Too complex."

"Then what are you betting on these days?"

"People pay me a lot of money for that information."

"It's an academic interest, Gordon. I just want to know what's going to happen after . . . well, later."

Gordon eyed me. "It's always safe to assume that it will be more of the same. Just faster, cheaper, and more out of control. Even the so-called black swans aren't really so unexpected any more. The Great Panic of 2023? I wasn't the only one to anticipate that happening. But everyone else assumed that catastrophe was safely in the distant future. I was the only one to put my chips down on double zero. The surprise is not that black swans exist. The surprise is when they decide to swim into view."[17]

"Are there any black swans swimming around just out of view that I should know about?"

"Well, I did hear something the other day about CRISPR International."

I felt my pulse quicken. "What was that?"

"Someone I know at Stanford sent me a very interesting and highly confidential report."

"Can you give me the gist?"

Gordon eyed me warily. "Why the sudden interest in CRISPR?"

"Oh, no reason really."[18]

"Apparently the company is testing a new drug."

"What kind of drug?"

"That's the confidential part, but it's a game-changer."

"Can you be more specific?"

Gordon suddenly looked to one side, paused for a few moments, and glanced back at me. "I'm sorry, Father, this is important. I have to take it."

---

17 Black swans, long assumed to be imaginary creatures, were discovered in Australia in the seventeenth century. They then came to signify very rare events with the potential of radically disrupting the status quo.

18 Gordon undoubtedly saw through this feigned nonchalance. Or it's possible that once again West is simply and conveniently misreporting the facts.

We were standing just outside the entrance to the pagoda. Gordon held up his hands apologetically, turned away, and started to talk in a low tone. His privacy settings were on high, his words encrypted. I couldn't have eavesdropped even if I'd known how to manipulate the VR apparatus far better than I did. As he talked, Gordon inscribed larger and larger circles around the pagoda.

The courtyard glowed in the darkness from hundreds of recessed lights. It was a peaceful space. I could hear the song of a thrush in a nearby tree. A couple was sitting on an ornately carved wooden bench, holding hands. A young man in a flowing crimson robe with a tightly braided queue that hung down to the middle of his back walked by me reading from an actual book. It had been years since I'd witnessed such a novelty. I thought about the violence and poverty of the city where I'd been living for the last decade. Gordon had bet on Ningxia, and I had to admit that it looked as though he'd backed the right horse.

I decided not to argue with him anymore. The purpose of my trip was not to reopen all the old wounds but to heal them, at least a few of them anyway. I wanted to hear his information about CRISPR. I also wanted to find out if he knew more about his brother's whereabouts. And perhaps Mei-hwa would live up to his enthusiastic reports. Perhaps they would give me a new grandchild, one whose birth I might actually witness.

When I looked up, though, I suddenly realized that Gordon was no longer in view. I took a few steps to the left and then to the right to see if I could find him under the colon-nade. Then I circled around the tower. I stepped through the gate of the courtyard to see if he was in the street. I switched to bird's-eye view and took in a four-block radius of the neighborhood.

My son had disappeared.

CHAPTER 4

In Gaborone

I lingered in Yinchuan City for an hour, waiting for Gordon to return or contact me. I sent multiple messages. I tried to find contact information for Mei-hwa West, but apparently she hadn't taken his last name, and there were too many Mei-hwas in Yinchuan to figure out which one might be my new daughter-in-law.[1] Gordon had never told me the name of the restaurant where we were to meet. I didn't even know if he worked in an office. It was shameful how little I knew about my middle child.

So I returned to bed. I didn't expect Gordon to send me a note of apology or explanation. He had always prioritized

---

[1] The name of Gordon's wife was actually Ming-hwa, and she did take his last name. It would have been reasonably uncomplicated to find her contact information, if West had remembered her name and recorded it correctly in his report.

business over family, a trait I seemed to have passed on to him. I took his disappearance to be just another of his reminders that turnabout was fair play.

I'd been surprised to hear that Benjamin was in Botswana. It was not his kind of country. Like Ningxia, Botswana was a rarity on the planet: a relatively stable and prosperous place. It was also, as I discovered after a quick infosearch, a small country with a largely black population concentrated in and around the capital city of Gaborone. I couldn't imagine it would be that difficult to find a white expat there.

Benjamin was our youngest. He had showed none of the precocity of his siblings, at least not in a fashion that my wife or I were capable of recognizing. He wasn't interested in intellectual matters or in making money, but he had great reserves of determination and concentration. He took an early interest in ants and could sit on his haunches in the backyard staring at them for hours. It's too bad that his testing-obsessed school beat that early entomological interest out of him. He would have made a marvelous scientist. It wasn't just his early fixation on ants that demonstrated his persistence. Like many children, he became a vegan when he learned the true origins of chicken fingers. But where other children were eventually seduced by a pepperoni pizza or an ice-cream cone, Benjamin made a lifelong commitment to eat nothing but vegetables, fruits, and grains.

He was, however, no willowy pacifist. From some recessive corner of our joint genetic stock, he had acquired the build of a heavyweight fighter. He had broad shoulders, stood more than two meters high, and possessed a set of muscles that he began working to develop as soon as he gained access to his middle school's gym. He applied himself to weightlifting, fitness training, and vegan protein powders with the same single-minded purpose he'd once directed toward those ant colonies. We successfully steered him away from the more dangerous sports—boxing, football—but our youngest liked to court danger. He threw himself into mountaineering and skiing. He went on survival expeditions that left him in the wilderness by himself for two weeks at a time with nothing but a compass and a granola bar. He became a devotee of various martial arts, focusing finally on Krav Maga, and advanced to a black belt when he was still in high school.

We were both taken by surprise when, at the dinner table one evening during the fall semester of his senior year, Benjamin announced that he was going to leave high school before graduation. It was 2019, and if I hadn't been distracted by the galleys of *Splinterlands*, I might have recognized all the warning signs.

"But it's just this one last year," my wife pleaded with him.

Benjamin shrugged. "I'm wasting my time here."

"In this economy, it's suicidal not to get a high school degree," I told him. "Even your brother Gordon—"

"I don't care about Gordon," he said. "I'm leaving next week."

My wife clenched her napkin. "Where are you going?"

"I'll send you all the information when I get there."

"We wouldn't dream of trying to stop you," I told my youngest son. "But there might be things we can do to help."

"I doubt it," he replied.

However, after some more prodding and a veiled threat or two, he did finally produce his plan. He was traveling alone to Turkey where he would connect with a representative from Kurdistan. They would smuggle him across the border to a training camp. He wanted to fight the Caliphate.

"It's the only moral thing to do right now," he informed us in breathless, impassioned tones. "This is a civilizational fight. You do realize this, don't you? I feel like this is what everything has been leading up to, all my training, all my preparations."

"Your commitment is admirable," I began.

My wife swallowed hard. "Wouldn't it be better if you acquired more training here before you go? Why don't you enlist in the Marines? The Navy SEALs? Then you could go over there in an official capacity."

"The fight is now, Mother. If we don't fight them right at this moment, they could win. Do you want them taking over Washington? Marching all the infidels onto the Mall and cutting off their heads? *Our* heads?"

"Of course not," I said. "But perhaps you're overestimating the threat."

Benjamin looked at me coldly, and I could suddenly see him with a weapon in his hands. "The wolf is at the door. I don't know why you can't hear it. But I hear it. And I know how hungry it is."[2]

It was canny of Benjamin to talk this way, for I had taught all of my children that civilization was but a thin crust wrapped around a molten core of savagery. Still, we spent the rest of the evening trying to reason with him. A young man with no language skills or experience in the region: We thought he was embarking on a suicide mission. But Benjamin was adamant. And in the end, we assured him that we would do everything we could to help him achieve his goal. After all, we found the Caliphate as abhorrent as he did.

But of course, when Benjamin arrived in Istanbul and attempted to rendezvous with his Kurdish contact, the Turkish police were waiting to arrest him. We hated the Caliphate, but we loved Benjamin more. We never told him that we were the ones to tip off the FBI, who then worked with their Turkish counterparts to pick him up. We never had the opportunity. But I'm sure that our son suspected us.

Our efforts were for naught. Benjamin was nothing if not resourceful. He overpowered his guards at the holding facility and escaped into Istanbul with nothing but the clothes he was wearing. From there, we lost track of him for several months. Finally, he sent a few untraceable messages to reassure us that he was okay. After that, the FBI occasionally provided us with updates about the exploits of

---

2 The reference here again is to *homo hominem lupus*. Benjamin is turning his father's words against him.

the mercenary who adopted the *nom de guerre* of Abu Jibril.[3] In turn, the Caliphate put a high price on his head. For one stretch of five years, the rumor was that he'd been betrayed and delivered over to the Caliphate's affiliate in Egypt.[4] I assumed he was dead and quietly mourned my son. My wife never gave up on him.

At the end of the 2030s, we each received a message, indirectly, that he was alive. He didn't want us to worry. He wished he could see us, but that wasn't possible.

Several years ago, a former academic colleague who studied the mercenary network in what had once been Iraq and Syria told me that Abu Jibril was no longer a fighter. He'd become a political operative, on the move constantly from one disintegrating country to another. It was no surprise, then, to learn from Aurora that Benjamin had taken up residence in Doha. It was a center of financing for the fight against the Caliphate. But I couldn't figure out why he would head for Botswana.

Certainly the Caliphate had established a number of successful branches throughout Africa—in Mali, Nigeria, and Sudan, among other places—anywhere with a significant Muslim population. But there were few Muslims in Botswana. And instead of being on the verge of disintegration,

---

3 Benjamin chose his name carefully, transforming himself into the emissary of the Angel Gabriel, who carried a message from God to the Caliphate: not paradise but death and eternal damnation.

4 This was a rumor that Benjamin himself circulated—in order to give himself more room for maneuver as he pursued his campaign against the Caliphate in North Africa.

that country was an oasis of stability on a chaotic continent. Unlike the top half of the continent, buried beneath the sands of the creeping Sahara, Botswana could still feed itself. It had money to buy whatever it couldn't grow. It had been lucky to discover rich deposits of diamonds in the 1960s, only a year *after* independence. With some more luck, it had managed to escape the resource curse that had torn apart other countries in a region rich in oil and minerals. The diamonds were now gone, but the country had invested the wealth wisely and was a center of financial services for the Global South. Perhaps my son had gone there on the trail of additional financing.

Or perhaps, and I dearly hoped this was true, he had decided to retire. After fighting for decades in a succession of failing states, Benjamin had gone to one of the few places in the world where he could sleep peacefully at night.

I once had an old-fashioned map on the wall in my office that showed all the places my son had fought, according to the scant information the FBI and others provided me. I never told my colleagues what the pushpins represented. They assumed it was a visual representation of *Splinterlands*. I found the correspondence deeply disturbing. For many years, I blamed myself for the eerie fact that my son's trajectory so closely followed the narrative of my bestseller.

But that was ridiculous. Benjamin left home a year before my book was published. He'd been at his most impressionable in 2014, when the Caliphate first emerged from the wreckage of the Middle East and before I'd even started thinking about writing *Splinterlands*. As centrifugal forces started to tear apart the great multiethnic states of the world—in a terrifying version of Yugoslavization that ricocheted across the planet—the Caliphate spread even as it morphed, changing its name as it absorbed victories and defeat, and Benjamin developed a passionate hatred for it. I later discovered that those initial beheadings by the Caliphate had affected him much as the immolation of Vietnamese monks or the 9/11 attacks had prodded young people of earlier generations into action.[5] As it happened, there was nothing I said or wrote that seems to have made much of an impression on him, then or subsequently. He'd made his decision to fight in the splinterlands before I even coined the term.

Some people did, however, read *Splinterlands* as a warning. Indeed, because of its speculative last chapter—which predicted more of the same fragmentation, but at an accelerated pace—critics began calling me the "Cassandra of catastrophe." I wasn't the first to warn of the world falling apart. Farseeing pundits, on the heels of the breakup of the Soviet Union and Yugoslavia, had predicted a wave of separatism in the 1990s. They were wrong only in terms of pace. And I was right primarily as a result of timing.

---

5 Unfortunately, Benjamin has, at least to date, not written a memoir, so it's almost impossible to understand his motivations. Aurora, in her book, describes her brother as an obsessive-compulsive who progressed from repeated hand washing to relentless weight lifting and finally to a life of Caliphate-fighting.

When *Splinterlands* appeared, the fissures in many countries were still small, sometimes barely visible. But in subsequent years they grew wider. In South Asia, separatist movements ate away at both India and Pakistan. In Southeast Asia, Indonesia, Malaysia, and Myanmar fractured along ethnic lines. In Africa, the center could not hold, and things inevitably fell apart—in the Congo, the Central African Republic, Nigeria, and Chad. In Latin America, a string of narco-states emerged, from Jalisco and Bahia to the overpopulated and hyperviolent Cortes.[6]

Throughout the Global South, national borders had been arbitrary to begin with, the result of colonial whim and imperialist greed. When these borders came under increasing strain, everything was soon up for grabs. The endless exploitation of vast underground riches, the influx of cheap weaponry, the failure of national identities to cohere, the proxy battles of superpowers: these all tore at countries that could often claim only a few decades of independence. A handful of outliers—Botswana, Bhutan, Belize—emerged from the unraveling relatively unscathed. Otherwise, the crumbling international community has yet to reach its angle of repose.

---

6 Interestingly, West leaves Antioquia off the list. Yet this narco-state, carved out of what was once Colombia, became the prototype for everything that happened in the region. Of course, Antioquia was also where the Central American Regional Security Initiative (CARSI) sent Isaac Kinbote to work undercover in 2019. Isaac had, by then, changed his name to Adam West and developed a new profile as a narco-trafficker. His reports remain classified, unfortunately, and could not be consulted for these annotations.

In the early twenty-first century, there was much talk of failed states like Afghanistan, Iraq, Somalia, Yemen, and Haiti. Looking back, it's now clear that, in a certain sense, all states were failing. From an evolutionary point of view, the state had played a useful function in mobilizing the energies of populations on behalf of a succession of economic revolutions—agrarian, industrial, digital—before ultimately proving as vestigial as tonsils or wisdom teeth. Even the seemingly strongest states stood little chance against the governance-eroding winds of globalization from above and the ever greater upheavals by nonstate actors below. The smaller states that emerged from the great shakeup were nothing like their predecessors. Except for the few examples Aurora had identified—Bavaria, Bretagne—they had little authority to raise revenue or guide an economy. They were either vehicles for the theft of natural resources or thin political camouflage for the generals, or both. The electorate collaborated in its own disenfranchisement. In the public's view, all politicians were corrupt, all civil servants inept, and every government little more than a Mafia plus an army. Once the public had been persuaded to cut the state down to size, the real Mafias took over.

In a way, my son was typical. He had little faith in the state and even less in multilateral institutions. He didn't want to submit to the discipline of a national army presided over by a commander-in-chief who answered to an indecisive electorate. He was itching to jump into the fray against the Caliphate, much as other young people, of a different persuasion, couldn't wait to sign up with the jihadis.

I should have been grateful that at least he'd chosen the right side.[7]

The day after Gordon abandoned me in Yinchuan City and after a fruitless attempt to track down Benjamin's whereabouts, I went directly to the Royal Palms Casino and Resort in Botswana's capital, Gaborone. It wasn't the sort of place I imagined Benjamin frequenting, but it seemed like the logical spot to begin.

The casino had a strict policy on avatars. We weren't allowed to enter the poker rooms lest we provide information covertly to players at the tables. We were forbidden from playing blackjack in case we had access to quantum computers to count cards. We were, however, free to wander in the rooms with the slot machines and the roulette tables. I could even gamble if I turned on my credit function and engaged a shadow to throw the dice or play the slots. This was all explained to me at the door by a large man sporting a tuxedo and mirrored retinal implants.

But I wasn't there to gamble. I headed directly to the bar to chat up likely sources of information. Within a few feet of the entrance, however, I found my way blocked as one "escort" after another offered me a variety of "entertainments."

---

7 West's confidence notwithstanding, it was not always easy to identify the sides in the conflict. A number of anti-Caliphate factions, for instance, had been part of the Caliphate before breaking away. According to the Terrorism Tracking Center, Benjamin's militia partnered over the years with some fairly disreputable actors.

"A distinguished gambler like yourself would surely be interested in rolling the dice with me," said one particularly alluring blonde in a see-through suit who offered to shadow me.

Shouldering her aside was a young man with rainbow cornrows down to his waist. "Or if you prefer, we could go to my room for some real shadow play."

After several fumbling attempts, I finally found the parental-control function on my apparatus and turned off the adult-content indicator, which I must have inadvertently triggered during the casino's admission process. Suddenly I was rendered invisible to the escorts and could make my way undisturbed to the bar.

I found a place next to a young man with mahogany skin and a smooth, shiny skull.

"I'm not interested," he said in English before I'd even opened my mouth.

"But you don't know what I want," I protested.

"I don't know how you got through my filters but whatever you're selling, I don't want it."

"I'm not—"

"Don't follow me," he growled as he pushed away from the bar, "or I'll call security."

I watched him merge into the crowd surrounding the craps table. I'd heard of such situations, where avatars functioned like walking, talking advertisements—all part of the new avatar economy. I turned back to the bar, deflated. This was going to be more difficult than I imagined.

Suddenly wishing I could order a drink to bolster my flagging confidence, I remembered the can of iced coffee I'd placed next to my bed. I groped for it as I continued to survey the casino. It was anything but easy to negotiate both worlds simultaneously, though my hand eventually came into contact with the metal can and I greedily drank its contents. When the caffeine hit my system, I instantly felt a decade younger.

The main room was crowded and noisy, the slot machines whirring and chirping. The crowds around the gaming tables periodically erupted in choruses of cheers and groans. Some kind of techno beat throbbed in the background. I hadn't been in such a place in years, but not much had changed, other than hairstyles and clothing.

"Is this your first sales trip?"

I turned around to find an older man looking at me. His skin was even darker than that of the fellow who'd snubbed me. A tightly coiled, grey-flecked Afro covered his scalp.

"I'm not on a sales trip," I confessed.

"Sometimes they send neophytes here to practice before tackling the real casinos, but you can be honest with me."

"I am being honest," I said. "I'm looking for somebody."

"An honest avatar?" the man asked, eyebrow arched. "Are you perhaps a private eye?"

"I'm looking for my son."

"I'm intrigued. Did he run away from home?"

"Some time ago," I said. "I thought he might show up in a place like this."

"To spend his inheritance?"

"Do you work here?" I asked.

"Well, yes, in a way." The man pressed his palm to his chest and inclined his head forward. "Adam Mogae. Minister of tourism."[8]

"Really?" I was flustered. "I'm sorry, I didn't—"

"No apologies necessary." He indicated a young woman at the craps table who was shaking her fist in the air before releasing the dice. "My wife. She's the gambler in the family."

His wife was beautiful. "You're a lucky man."

"I suppose I am."

I extended my hand, then realized that avatars didn't introduce themselves that way. I copied his gesture by putting a palm on my own chest and bowing slightly. "I'm Julian West."

"A pleasure," he said, smiling broadly. "Now, about your son."

"He's probably here under an assumed name."

"Undoubtedly."

"And I don't really know what he's doing here."

"Laying low, I suppose," Adam Mogae said. "There aren't that many tourists here in the capital. Most are up north, on safari in the Okavango. Still, you'll have difficulty finding your son unless you have some scrap of information."

I quickly combed through what I knew about Benjamin,

---

8 Mogae was not merely the minister of tourism; he was also a descendent of one of Botswana's first presidents, Festus Mogae, who served two terms from 1998 to 2008. In other words, he was very well connected and West extraordinarily fortunate to run into him. Unless, of course, it wasn't a coincidence.

which wasn't much. I didn't even know what he looked like any more. The only photos of Abu Jibril were shadowy shots of a man turning away from the camera. "I know where he probably came from. Doha. Within the last two weeks."

The man slapped his palm on the bar counter. "Excellent! That should narrow things down nicely. Let's go."

"Go? Where?"

"To my car. I have access to our airport's surveillance footage from there."

"But your wife?"

"She probably won't even notice that I'm gone. This will only take a few minutes."

And indeed, that's all the time it took for Adam Mogae, sitting with me in his chauffeured hovercar behind the casino, to scan through the several hundred passengers who'd entered Botswana in the last two weeks en route from Doha. Only one of these fit my description of Benjamin. His name was Jude MacAbee, flying on a Scottish passport. I didn't recognize the man whose face had been captured by the surveillance camera. But when I asked Adam Mogae to increase the magnification, I recognized the tiny scar on the left earlobe, the result of an early snowboarding accident. Mogae conducted a few more searches and provided me with Jude MacAbee's hotel information.

"You've been so helpful," I said. "And you don't even know me at all."

"Ah, but I do," Mogae said, his face lighting up. "As soon as I saw you at the bar, I thought I recognized you from your author's photo. *Splinterlands* was a bible for me when I was a young man. I'd like to think that your book helped us here in Botswana avoid many of the problems that have afflicted the rest of the world."

"You are too kind." It had been years since I'd been recognized in this way.[9]

"One word of warning," Mogae said, as we got out of his car. "When I accessed the surveillance system, I saw a flag. Someone tried to hack our systems yesterday. That's not something ordinarily worthy of concern, but they were also interested in passengers coming from Doha."

"Were they successful?"

"No. But watch your back, my friend."

VR has a function that specifically allows you to watch your back. But still I felt uneasy.

I went directly to the Hotel President, where my son was staying. Overlooking a square of banks in the downtown area, it had seen better days. The red carpet in the lobby was frayed and the lighting dim. I could almost smell the mustiness in the air. I slipped some credit to the hotel manager, along with a story about being on my first sales trip. He let me sit unmolested in the lobby. I spent several hours watching the clientele—budget-class tourists from the Balkans, South Asia, and other parts of Africa passing a night in the capital before heading off to bag an eland or

---

9 West is not indulging in false modesty. Once a required text in many academic disciplines, *Splinterlands* has become a classic that virtually no one reads any more.

two in the north. It was a good place for a mercenary to hide. I wasn't sure what I would do when I saw my son. But I knew I had to be careful. If I tipped him off in any way, I would never be able to find him again.

The iced coffee proved useful. I'd suspected that I would have to stay awake for a long period to locate my son. And it did indeed take a long time. There was, moreover, little to engage my attention. I watched tourists make assignations with escorts, second-tier business reps strike deals, and a pair of North Korean diplomats sell what appeared to be a bag of rhino horns.[10] I read news bits on an old large-screen e-reader that the hotel provided the few guests who lacked retinal implants. From the updates, I learned of a coordinated series of Sleeper attacks across North America. Scientists were predicting a seaweed shortage by the end of the decade and "greater food insecurity" as a result, which meant yet more famine for the poorest of the poor. Cases of a strange new staph infection were cropping up and no longer just in the elderly population—but the World Health Organization couldn't secure sufficient agreement from its members to launch a coordinated response. Climate-change refugees in an offshore facility in the In-

---

10 The diplomats would in fact be expelled from Botswana not long afterward for "trafficking in contraband." Despite perennial predictions of collapse, North Korea even today has managed to avoid the centrifugal forces that have torn apart so many other countries. West wrote an essay on the "North Korean exception" to his thesis that I critiqued in my contribution to the panel on Northeast Asia at the Fifteenth Association of Geo-Paleontologists Conference.

dian Ocean had managed to overpower center administrators and were now demanding recognition as New Island. And in local news, another luxury resort community was opening up in what had once been the Kalahari Desert, but was now a temperate oasis, thanks to global warming.

The coffee was beginning to wear off when, around 4 a.m., Benjamin sauntered into the lobby surrounded by an entourage of several men and women. I was positioned in such a way that I could observe him without being observed, the e-reader in front of my face but the VR's bird's-eye view switched on. I immediately recognized the rolling gait of my youngest son. Ever since he'd taken up martial arts as a teenager, he walked as if the ground beneath his feet pitched like the deck of a ship in a storm.

I waited a few minutes after the entourage passed before making my way to the fourth-floor room where I knew Benjamin was staying. I thought I'd taken sufficient precautions. But as soon as I stepped from the stairwell into the corridor, I froze. Literally.

At first I thought it was a glitch in the system. I went through the motions that I had learned to unstick my avatar. When that didn't work, I tried to reboot. But I couldn't, nor, I soon discovered, could I pull the apparatus off my head. My arms seemed paralyzed. I couldn't move in either of the two dimensions in which I was operating. And that's when I started to sweat.

"Kill him?" asked a Castilian-accented voice behind me in the hotel corridor. "He's obviously an amateur."

"Wait."

A figure appeared before me. It was Benjamin. I tried to speak but couldn't open my mouth.

"The hotel manager says he was sitting there for six hours," the Castilian said.

Benjamin was looking intently but impassively at my face. "No, don't kill him. At least, not yet. Send him to your room. I want to talk to him there. Alone."

"You know him?"

"Send him to your room. And put two people at the door. Just in case."

I was propelled involuntarily down the corridor. Somehow they had seized control of my apparatus and its navigation system. Worse, they had somehow hacked into my own nervous system. I lay paralyzed in my bed, unable to lift a finger to help my avatar as it was transported like a large valise to a hotel room and set down on the floor between two twin beds.

Benjamin followed me into the room. He spoke to one of the people at the door, and I suddenly felt a small amount of freedom restored to me. I still couldn't manipulate my real body, but my avatar had regained the power of speech.

My son closed the door. He held a device up in the air and seemed to scan the room with it. He looked at the readings. Satisfied, he put the device back into his pocket.

"Wide is the gate, Benjamin?" I asked.

"We're safe now." He turned to me. "Who sent you, Father?"

"No one."

"I haven't seen you in more than thirty years. And you suddenly show up in Botswana? How did you even find out that I was here?"

"Gordon."

"And how did he know I was here?"

"I don't know."

"This is important, Father. Please remember."

"He didn't say."

Benjamin was pacing back and forth. "This is not good."

"Is it the Caliphate? Is that why you're here?"

"No. The Caliphate is over."

"Really?" I was surprised. "But the Sleepers?"

"Dead men walking. We recently destroyed the central command. The Sleepers haven't yet gotten the message. There will still be suicide attacks. But it should tail off in a year or so."[11]

"That's why you left Doha? Have you retired? Is the fight over?"

"Not exactly."

"But haven't you fought enough?"

Benjamin folded his arms across his chest. He was now nearly fifty and had grown into an imposing man.

---

11 Benjamin's prediction regarding the Caliphate was largely correct. What he didn't anticipate—or at least didn't mention to his father—was the emergence of another millenarian movement that appealed to much the same base and inspired a comparable backlash. By this point, however, Benjamin had already shifted his focus.

His neck was thick, and even through his loose shirt I could see the outlines of his muscled body. Deep lines radiated from the corners of his eyes, which made him look tired and anxious. "Retire? What do you think I do, Father? Give lectures on counterterrorism with a little import-export on the side? There's no retirement in my profession."

"A lot of freedom fighters in history have become respected members of society: Nelson Mandela, Gerry Adams, Yitzhak Rabin."

"Is that why you're here? To continue the argument we had on the last night we saw each other?"

"I'm revisiting *Splinterlands*. To prepare a report."

"A report?" Benjamin laughed bitterly. "You predicted that the world would go to shit. It went to shit. And this is going to be your I-told-you-so report?"

"I'm trying to figure out *why* it went to shit."

"That's an easy one."

"Well?"

"Because there were more people like you. And fewer people like me."

"People who think with their fists rather than their heads?"

"People willing to fight a clear and present danger. That's what I told you thirty years ago. The tigers of wrath are wiser than the horses of instruction, Father."

"But you were just fighting the symptoms. You never addressed the root causes. As long as those root causes still exist, the Caliphate will just pop up again somewhere else."

"You know nothing about what we've done over the last thirty years." Benjamin was obviously angry, but he didn't let it affect his tone. Only the characteristic flaring of his nostrils gave him away. "The terrible sacrifices we made."

"I know that poverty and injustice still exist."

"They've always existed," Benjamin said. "There are always going to be root causes. And if you use that argument as an excuse for inaction, you'll soon find yourself in line for the gas chambers. Because these 'symptoms' of yours have real weapons and kill real people."

"But it wasn't your fight," I insisted. "It wasn't a fight between Islam and the West. It was a fight within Islam."[12]

"And you think you're telling me something I don't already know? Just because it was a fight within Islam doesn't mean that it wasn't my fight too. We were up against pure evil. Or perhaps you take the view that evil doesn't exist."

"Violence begets violence."

He shook his head. "You came a long way to spout clichés."

"Why don't you come home for a visit? Your mother would like to see you once more before she dies."

The years fell away, and he suddenly looked vulnerable. "Is she sick?"

"Yes," I lied.

---

12 In *Splinterlands*, West wrote, "The debate over the so-called 'clash of civilizations' obscured an essential point: Most of the clashes in the Middle East were taking place *within* civilizations. Within Islam, for instance, Shia battled Sunni. And the Wahhabi fundamentalists clashed with their Sunni coreligionists on essential questions of doctrine and practice."

He looked to the side and then, after a moment, back to me. "There's no evidence of that on the Arcadian channels."

"But she wants to see you."

"I still have work to do here."

"What work?"

"It's better if you don't know."

"Maybe I can help."

"Like you helped when I went off to Turkey and you contacted the FBI?"

I took a deep breath. "We did what we thought was best for you."

"And you were wrong."

"What we did . . . *was* wrong. I see that now."

Benjamin looked down at his hands. "I'm glad to hear that."

"Tell me how I can help you now."

"You can't help me. We're fighting a very different battle now."

"But what kind of battle is taking place here in Botswana? Is the country finally going the way of the rest of Africa?"

"Oh no, Botswana is still a very stable country. It's an attractive place for a different kind of predator."

"And what does this have to do with the Caliphate?"

"I told you—it has nothing to do with the Caliphate. Threats to civilization come in many different packages."

"What kind of predator?"

"I've already told you too much."[13]

"Please, I . . . I want to help."

"You can help by leaving. And not coming back. Give my love to mother."

"Wait, Benjamin, I—"

But his face dissolved into grey, and I was again back in my own bed.

---

13 It's intriguing that Benjamin said anything to his father, given the earlier betrayal. It suggests that Benjamin might have known why his father was there and was hoping to extract useful information from him. It's also possible that he had arranged for Adam Mogae to intercept his father at the casino. Repeated requests for information from Minister Mogae's office have been ignored.

CHAPTER 5

In Arcadia

Though I had regained the use of my own limbs, I lay in my bed for many hours, motionless. I had thought that, as an observer, I could use the VR apparatus to wander safely no matter how dangerous the territory. After all, I'd watched a bloody battle in South Brussels and suffered nothing worse than brief hyperventilation. Now, however, I no longer felt protected, and what Benjamin had told me was even more disturbing. What was the new threat that he was determined to fight?

Distraught as I was, I missed my appointment with my ex-wife. She messaged me, concerned. I was usually so punctual. She immediately jumped to the conclusion that I'd fallen ill, and in a way, she was right. As she so often is.

To fortify myself, I pulled another can of iced coffee from the unit beneath my bed. My condition seemed to be spreading from my feet up my legs. I didn't know how much time I had left, but it wasn't a good sign. I put the VR apparatus back on and prepared to embark on my last trip.

I'd met Rachel when she was a graduate student and I was just starting at my first teaching job in Cambridge, Massachusetts. It was 1994, and I was so filled with hope. The Cold War had ended. The threat of nuclear annihilation had been lifted. I'd just published my book on European integration, and I truly thought that Brussels represented the future of humanity. Of course, others gazed upon the peace and prosperity of Europe and deemed it the end of history altogether—as if history consisted only of bloody struggle and the glory that the combatants derived from it. In those days, I dismissed the fratricidal dissolution of Yugoslavia, the breakdown of order in Somalia, and the genocide in Rwanda as aberrations. Later I came to understand that they prefigured the future in a way that the endless meetings of the Eurocrats I studied with the devotion of a sports fanatic didn't.[1]

Rachel didn't share my early optimism, which was not surprising since her subject was climate change. Perhaps that's why I was so attracted to her. We were such very different creatures. When I met her, Rachel Leopold was studying the effects of global warming on the Arctic. She was a student of ice. And I suppose you could say that I eventually became a student of fire. Maybe we weren't made

---

1 For a study of this period of transition in West's thinking, see for instance Richard Caplan, *From Student of Integration to Apostle of Disintegration: Julian West and the Making of* Splinterlands (Linacre College Press, 2029).

for each other, but in those early days we were certainly mad for each other. Later, what we produced in common—our children—held us together. When they left, our mutual love for literature and disdain for the meretricious weren't sufficient to keep us together. We retreated into our elemental natures. She froze up and I burned out of control. But that came later, much later.

After Rachel finished her graduate work, we eventually secured two academic appointments in the Washington area and set up our household in the District. We raised our three children, born across an increasingly hectic six-year period, even as we wrote books and gave papers at conferences. We hosted dinner parties that mingled colleagues from our respective departments. Living inside the Beltway, we gave our share of briefings on the Hill but never considered ourselves part of that milieu. We nurtured a community of like-minded friends. In this affinity group, reinforced by what we read and the networks we created on social media, we complained about the polarization of politics, the pervasive influence of lobbyists, and the rise of fanatical homegrown fundamentalists.

We were academics. We were critical. We were happy.

Or so I thought.

During those years of raising a family and jumping through the requisite academic hoops, I watched the world go to pieces, believing like so many Americans that my country was an exception to the rule. We elected our first African American president way back in 2008 and repaired

America's international reputation, which had been so damaged by the previous eight years of hypermilitarism. We survived the financial crisis of 2007 and 2008. We instituted national healthcare. We began to address climate change. We made peace with Iran and Cuba.

But it turned out that these were half-measures. The wars continued under different names in Iraq and Afghanistan, there were additional interventions in places like Libya and Syria, and our drones initiated a strange new arms race. For every step forward on international policy, the United States took two steps back in its failure to address the global crises that would ultimately dwarf all prior disagreements over turf and tenet.

Many commentators in those years likened the predicament of humanity to that of the proverbial frog in the pot of boiling water, suggesting that we weren't taking notice of the incremental increase in the temperature of our surroundings until it was too late. But the metaphor was imprecise. After all, we filled the pot with water, put it on the stove, turned up the heat, and then willingly dove into this hot tub of our own making—after which we pretended that we were poor frog victims, helpless and hapless. Meanwhile, the real frogs, species after species, were dying off at an alarming rate—again, thanks to us—and we barely paid attention. The frog-in-a-pot metaphor did, however, capture a key component of the crisis: complacency.

I remember reading an article at the time that warned of a "Goldilocks apocalypse" in which the world wouldn't end with a bang or a whimper but, rather, with a comfortable sigh of self-satisfaction.[2] And that, it turned out, was indeed the fate of the United States. Because it refused to engage in a more radical restructuring, it fell victim to the same splintering as the rest of the world.

The first to go was not the United States itself but the American empire. True, Washington didn't preside over a classic empire. It was, as the political scientists once liked to say, more of a hegemonic order, in which our client states thought that they were doing what they wanted to do rather than what they were bidden to do. During the 2000s, I watched as this order began to collapse. Other centers of power emerged: China, Russia, India, Brazil. The European Union briefly took center stage as a major foreign-policy actor before succumbing to its own internal distractions and fragmentation. Meanwhile, the United States spent itself into enormous debt to maintain a huge military, even as it opposed any attempt to create a more equitable international political structure that could have superseded the nation-state system.

---

2 In this somewhat tendentious essay, the author writes, "We seek out the comfortable middle at our own peril. Not too hot and not too cold, not too hard and not too soft, it's a strategy guaranteed to lull anyone into a dangerous complacency. After all, once you've made your bed, however comfortable it may be, you have to lie in it. And it's then, after a few brief moments of self-satisfied sleep, that you're bound to hear the scratching at the door. The bears are home. And they're hungry." This passage clearly influenced West's thinking and even his writing style, as later sections of this report indicate.

At home, it self-destructively refused to invest in the country's decaying infrastructure, enabling foreign hackers and homegrown terrorists to exploit weaknesses in transportation and communication networks, causing several embarrassing and costly stoppages. In 2023, when the dollar fell from its perch as a global currency, the US government went into receivership and its vast overseas military footprint became unsupportable. As it withdrew, Washington deputized its allies—Germany, Japan, South Korea, Saudi Arabia, Israel—to do the same work, but they regularly operated at cross-purposes and in any case began to fragment themselves, beginning with the secessions of Okinawa, Bavaria, and Saudi Arabia's Eastern Province in the mid-2020s.

Meanwhile, domestic politics remained divided as Congress and the executive branch congealed like two pots of cold oatmeal. Neither they nor the various states of the union could establish a consensus on how to re-energize the economy or reconceive the "national interest." Up went higher walls to keep out foreigners and foreign products. With the exception of military affairs and immigration control, the government's role dwindled to that of caretaker. The country experienced an epidemic of mega-assault rifles, armed personal drones, and weaponized biological agents, all easily downloaded at home on 3D printers. Though many refused to acknowledge the trend, our society drifted into a condition closely approximating psychosis.[3] An increasingly

---

3 *Splinterlands* received some criticism for West's occasional application of popular psychology to geopolitics. See, for example, Karin Lee, "Diag-

embittered and armed white minority seemed determined to adopt a scorched-earth policy rather than leave anything of value to its mixed-race heirs.[4] Today, of course, the country exists in name only, for the policies that really matter are all enacted on a local basis.

In the new era of climate change, which hastened the fracturing of the planet, Hurricane Donald should not have been a surprise. Hurricane Katrina's devastation of the Gulf Coast in 2005 had been a foretaste. Then came the earthquake and tsunami combination that wiped out a large portion of Oregon in 2019. But the politicians and financiers didn't really care about those disasters "on the margins." When disaster struck the capital, however, the visuals were shocking. No one ever expected to see those images of people clinging to the base of the Statue of Freedom atop the US Capitol. The waters submerged the Supreme Court, the White House, the Pentagon, and everything else in what had once been the low-lying swamps between Maryland and

nosing the Diagnostician: Julian West's Misuse of Psychology," *Journal of Social Work*, January 2022.

4 Here and there in the text are suggestions of West's guilt over his treatment of his first son, Isaac Kinbote, his "mixed-race heir." As we know from a variety of other sources, including his daughter Aurora's memoir, West initially refused to acknowledge his paternity of Isaac. He claimed in his early letters to Isaac's mother that she "was sleeping around the entire time we were married." An obvious family resemblance, confirmed by a later DNA test, forced him to admit that Isaac was indeed his son. Even then, he provided very little in the way of monthly payments to the family. When his material circumstances improved, nothing changed. That he sent anything at all he never revealed to his second wife and family, until, of course, that ill-fated cruise to Nova Scotia in 2021.

Virginia. Nature had provided America with the long-term loan of that swampland, and in 2022, it suddenly called that loan due.

Religious extremists of all faiths declared that Donald was a sign from a vengeful God who wanted to cleanse the country of its corrupt politicians, liberal Supreme Court justices, and gun-fearing, marijuana-loving DC residents.[5] Antigovernment activists, who had been occupying federal buildings and creating survivalist compounds beyond the reach of the authorities, were delighted that dirty water swept away what they'd always considered to be dirty in the first place. The United States didn't fall apart that year, as the political and religious fundamentalists predicted, but the process had begun.

After Hurricane Donald, Rachel decided to leave academia. This choice astonished me. She could have gotten a tenured position at practically any university here or abroad. The job I'd arranged for her at the University of Nebraska would have matched her Georgetown salary and then some. But at the age of fifty-one, she left all that behind, moved to Vermont, and joined a commune.

"This is the 2020s!" I shouted over the phone from my new apartment in Omaha. "It's not the 1960s!"

"You're the geo-paleontologist," she said. "All the big things are dying out. The logical thing is to go small."

---

5 This was, in fact, the subject of my first academic publication: Emmanuel Puig, "Apocalypse Deferred: Hurricane Donald and Religious Millenarianism," *Journal of Geo-Paleontology*, April 2032, 23–42.

"Just because big is doomed doesn't mean that small is beautiful."

"I'd like to test that proposition."

"But you're running away!"

"Says the man who ran off to the middle of Nebraska."

"But I didn't come here to stick my head in the sand."

"I suspect that you're sticking your head somewhere else. But I don't want to presume."

"So does that mean it's over?"

"We can talk about your joining me here. Under certain conditions."

"Give up everything and become a neo-tribalist at my age?"

"The hurricane did us a favor. We both have considerably less to give up."

"But I don't want to lose you, too!"

"Dear Julian, you've been losing me for years."[6]

The commune, called Arcadia, was located in the rolling mountains of what used to be called the Northeast Kingdom of Vermont, not far from the border with Quebec. It had been stitched together from two working dairy farms and several former vacation homes. Rachel had joined not long after its inception, when it was still growing. One of its founding principles was equilibrium. New members were accepted when the departure rate (by death or choice) exceeded the birth rate. Most of the children of the original

---

6 It's difficult to pinpoint when the relationship began to fray. Certainly matters came to a head during the fateful cruise to Nova Scotia.

members had, however, stayed in the community to assume
the responsibilities of their parents.

Rachel joined and never left, except for the occasional
trip to see our grandchildren in Brussels. She was now in
her late seventies. Her face had a weathered look, and her
long grey hair was gathered into a plait. But she had aged
gracefully. Her spine was straight, and she seemed to walk
without any difficulties. Never particularly voluble, she had
adopted the clipped cadence and even some of the swallowed consonants of Vermonters. She was and yet wasn't
the woman I'd wooed and won more than half a century before. Although she was cool to me now after meeting again
after so many years, I could still discern the spark that had
once attracted me.

Instead of sitting us down for a heart-to-heart, she immediately took me on a tour of Arcadia—as if I were a prospec-
tive member rather than the ex-husband she hadn't seen
in twenty-five years. Our first stop was the plastic-sheathed
greenhouses lined up like a dozen barracks along a stream
that ran through the property. She was, she explained, in
charge of vegetable production. Once a competent gar-
dener, she had clearly become a professional over the last
quarter-century. The diversity of production was dazzling. I
counted ten different kinds of squash, seven different pep-
pers, and a kaleidoscopic range of tomatoes. Rachel gave
me a mini-lecture about seed-saving, heirlooms, and the
dangers of genetic engineering. I was mesmerized by seeing so many real vegetables in one place.

"It's a gold mine here," I finally said.

"Our diet is very healthy," she replied. "No processed food. No seaweed."

"And it's all consumed here?"

"We barter with the neighbors, and we get the things from the general store we can't grow or manufacture—salt, nails, fabric."

"Sugar?"

"Beehives."

"Flour?"

"We grind our own."

"Fertilizer?"

"The cows and chickens produce plenty. Plus we have composting toilets. We've broken the fatal link between fossil fuels and agriculture. I'll show you the windmills. We're not Luddites. All our buildings are covered in solar paint."

Arcadia was largely self-sufficient: If push came to shove, the community could survive without outside help. Locals and a few flatlanders had commandeered several other abandoned farmsteads nearby to create comparable communes. Together, they formed a kind of trading confederation. Here was my European Union in miniature. Perhaps they would someday set up a parliament and a court to rival or replace what the Republic of Vermont and New Hampshire had already established.[7]

---

7 That has yet to happen. Arcadia is still functioning, but many of the other communes have failed.

Finally, after expressing my admiration for yet another row of overproducing plants, I tried to steer the conversation to matters closer to home.

"I saw our children," I told her. "They send their love."

"We've been in touch."

"Have you heard from Aurora recently?"

"Last week."

I decided not to tell her about my experience in Brussels. There was no reason to make her anxious. "I also saw Benjamin."

That got her attention. For years, "our children" had meant only Aurora and Gordon. Even when we were reasonably certain that Benjamin was still alive, it was as if we'd given him up for adoption at an advanced age. He had, after all, joined a very different family.

"Is he okay?" she asked, a slight tremor in her voice.

"He seems healthy. And he's no longer in the game, so to speak. Or rather, he's in a different game. I saw him in Botswana."

"Why Botswana?"

"I'm not really sure, but he's no longer fighting the Caliphate."

"Is he with someone?"

I thought, yes, of course, our son is with an entourage of armed thugs. But then I realized that she meant something entirely different. "I don't know."

"I hope he's found someone," she said. "He was always such a lonely boy."

"I never considered Benjamin the married-with-children type."

"It doesn't have to be that way," she said. "Just someone to share his dreams."

I wanted to ask Rachel if she, too, had found someone to share her dreams. How many intimate relationships had she developed on this commune? Or had she finally settled, like I had, into personal self-sufficiency?

I imagined for a moment what it might have been like to have followed Rachel instead of insisting that she follow me. I'm not particularly good with my hands, but I could have done something suitably white-collar at the commune, like keeping the accounts or serving as the community librarian. Perhaps I could have transferred my knowledge of how some institutions endure and others fail. In that way, I might have avoided any number of mistakes in my life—the five-year ordeal with Mary, the ugly leave-taking from the University of Nebraska, the scandal in Istanbul that nearly ended my career.[8]

Counter-history is always a temptation. Imagine, say, catching that train instead of missing it by a few seconds: how different life could have been.[9] I've long considered

---

8 West underplays this scandal. What took place at the Twentieth Association of Geo-Paleontologists Conference effectively ended his career. See Emmanuel Puig, *The Decline of West: Julian West, Isaac Kinbote, and the Scandalous Origins of Geo-Paleontology* (Smoking Gun, 2051).

9 On his trip to Kingston, Jamaica, during his college years, West just missed a ferry to Port Royal. Instead, he ended up getting a drink at the bar at the ferry terminal—and there he met Alesha Kinbote. He

my last extended phone conversation with Rachel in 2023 to be the decisive pivot around which my life turned. I've replayed it so many times that I'm no longer sure if it bears any resemblance to the actual conversation. But no matter how often I've pushed rewind, I never figured out a way to convincingly rewrite the script. The fact of the matter is, I simply wouldn't have abandoned academia to retire to a Vermont commune before I'd hit sixty. As far as I was concerned, I hadn't come close to finishing my contributions to the field and wasn't ready to put myself out to pasture.

This report—this sequel to *Splinterlands*—is also a nod in the direction of counter-history. I hope to identify the fateful crossroads where humanity made the wrong turn, where it could have embarked on a forking path to a very different future.[10]

For decades, scholars have put the onus on large imper-sonal events—Hurricane Donald, the Great Panic of 2023, the displacement of the dollar—as if a policy nudge or two one way or another might have prevented these develop-ments. I've always focused instead on 2018. As far as I can tell, that was the last moment when we had a definite shot at dodging the bullet.

---

must often have wondered how his life might have been different if he'd caught that ferry.

10 This passage suggests that West intended to structure this report quite differently, devoting a significant part of the narrative to a description of the course of history had humanity taken a different path. Naturally, all this changed when he had to rush to complete the manuscript.

The problem is: It wasn't a single bullet and there wasn't a single gun. If several EU countries hadn't set up internal borders against refugees, migrant workers, and perceived terrorists, if the United States hadn't made one last effort to preserve its global military "footprint," if the world community hadn't paid mere lip service to its previous commitments to curb carbon emissions, the story might have turned out differently.

Or at least I'd like to believe that. But if I can't imagine choosing the other option with my wife on one fairly straightforward issue, how could I believe that the great aircraft carrier of history might actually have changed course?

In the end, such speculation is idle, particularly for a geo-paleontologist. The only pertinent question is whether the knowledge of past error can actually help guide decisions in the present. As a member of that vanishing breed of progressives, I still firmly believe that we can learn from our mistakes. But sometimes, late at night here in my hospital bed, I fear that we are condemned to repeat the past regardless of whether we remember it or not. I don't doubt that we still have convictions. We just don't seem to have the requisite courage to follow them.

"We can triple crop outside now that we've become a Zone Nine region," Rachel was saying as we left the greenhouses. "We produce more food than we can eat."[11]

---

11 Vermont had been located for centuries in Zone Four. Rapid warming had transformed it into the California of the East, even as the fertile valleys of California were turning into arid wastelands.

"What about water?"

"The draw is good. But in twenty-five years we might have some problems. No snow any more in the mountain ranges. The Tibetans say: When the mountains wear black hats, the world will end."

"But some new technology will probably come along."

"Don't count on it."

"If solar paint hadn't—"

"Green swans," she interjected with a contemptuous laugh.

"I've heard of black swans, but—"

"We'll be saved by some as-yet-to-be-invented technology? It's an intellectual construct that allows us to continue our wastrel ways. In other words, we're talking about something so unlikely as to be imaginary, hence a green swan."

"But we've had some unimaginable technological advances. Gene splicing, for instance."

"They haven't saved us. Our grandparents would have been amazed that you're able to visit me right now from the comfort of your own armchair. But it hasn't stopped one half of humanity from cutting off the heads of the other half. It hasn't stopped the global temperature from rising."

"Not yet, perhaps, but—"

"Those Martian colonists think that they'll do better out there? They're bringing all the deadly diseases of Earth with them."[12]

---

12 Rachel is referring to the Plan B colony, established on Mars in 2035. It lasted for only twenty years, despite several resupply missions. The popularity of various conspiracy theories notwithstanding, a combination

"They've carefully screened out TB, all communicable diseases—"

"Greed? Aggression? Arrogance?"

"Then why are you even bothering with Arcadia?" I countered impatiently. "Or have you figured out how to keep out those particular diseases?"

Rachel shrugged. "I just don't have much faith in the future. That's why we're seeing if turning back the clock will achieve something different."

We were passing by an orchard that sloped up and away from us until it merged with the surrounding forest. I stared at the fruit-laden branches. "But you can't turn the clock back all the way to—"

"Eden?" Rachel plucked a low-hanging orange. She offered it to me. "You've probably forgotten what one of these really tastes like. Ah, I forgot. You're not really here." She unwrapped the skin of the orange in one long spiral. After carefully tucking the peel in the breast pocket of her plaid shirt, she began to eat the fruit, section by section. After she was halfway through, she said, "Now I only trust what's right in front me. That's the ultimate dividing line between us. You were always one for big generalizations."

"I always tried to build my generalizations on the solid foundation of accumulated facts."

"Naturally." She spat out a pip.

---

of technical malfunctions and community tensions ultimately doomed the colony (not, for instance, a bacterial infection introduced by a disgruntled former corporate sponsor).

"And you didn't indulge in generalizations? What is climate change if not a generalization?"

"Quite the contrary. Climate change was the ice that was slipping through my very fingers. Theories didn't interest me. Theories that great technological advances would save us? Theories that artificial intelligence would doom us? What nonsense. We had a threat right before our eyes. And we needed to take action."

"But action has to proceed from a theory."

Rachel groaned. "Must we?"

"It's just that, well—"

"I did something. I came here."

I plunged ahead, heedlessly. "But you could have done so much more as a scientist. To persuade governments to change their policies. You could have had a global impact."

"Don't you think that the statute of limitations has run out on that argument?"[13]

"But it wasn't too late, even after Hurricane Donald, to—"

"You don't get it, do you, Julian? I talked and I talked and I talked. And it didn't do anything. It was like shouting into the winds of Hurricane Donald. No one was listening. Certainly not you. You could have helped us build something here. But you had bigger ambitions."

She was right. *Splinterlands* made me an international celebrity, albeit of a minor intellectual variety. And I wasn't about to give that up by escaping to Vermont. I had cre-

---

13 They were indeed going over the same ground they had covered in the fateful phone call in which Rachel announced her intention to join Arcadia.

ated an entirely new discipline. I was invited all over the world—Moscow, Beijing, Cape Town—to help universities set up their own geo-paleontology programs. Even though my book peered into the recent past, it proved unusually prescient. One after another, the dinosaurs went extinct, and with each extinction my reputation grew. Arcadia was a bushel in the Vermont countryside, and I didn't want to hide my light beneath it.[14]

If *Splinterlands* had a blind spot, it was climate change. I was married to a glaciologist, yet somehow I didn't really anticipate the massive impact of climate change on the Great Unraveling. I should have shared the manuscript with Rachel. I was simply in too much of a rush to get it published. And she was busy with her own projects. When she wasn't taking ice samples in the Arctic, she was teaching, testifying before Congress, or working with NGOs.

I made the mistake of thinking that climate change was "out there" like avian flu or nuclear weapons: a potential vector of future destruction rather than a fundamental disorder at the heart of the modern system. In fact, climate

---

14 West is not just talking about his decision not to move to Arcadia. He is also referring, however indirectly, to his decision to conceal his "other family," which ultimately made it very difficult for him to move to Arcadia even if he had so desired. When Isaac Kinbote turned eighteen and Alesha wrote to ask if West would sponsor their son at a US university, he refused. He didn't want to risk having Isaac anywhere near Washington. Instead, he offered to pay for Isaac's education in Jamaica or anywhere else in the region. Meanwhile, he managed to keep knowledge of the existence of the Kinbotes from Rachel and his other children until the Nova Scotia cruise in 2021.

change was re-engineering the very DNA of the global order. Water wars helped split China apart. Energy conflicts remapped the Middle East, Central Asia, and Africa. Arable land became so precious that several rich agricultural regions—Centro-Sul in Brazil, Java in Indonesia—secured their independence in order to fence off their territory.

In the end, climate change had the last laugh. "So, you don't believe we're important?" the weather gods boomed from behind the gathering clouds. "Let's see what you think about this!" And the heavens opened, and the rains poured down, and my world filled up with water.

Despite my failure to anticipate the full effects of climate change, the world fell apart just as I predicted. At such a moment when governments were seeking my advice, media were clamoring for my commentary, and universities were competing for my affections, I had no intention of burying myself in a commune in the middle of nowhere. Then, shortly after moving to Omaha, I met Mary, who proved as compelling at the beginning of our relationship as she was repellent by its end.[15] I was so focused on my work, on my new lover, on traveling the world on well-paid consultancies, that I lost track of my family. Even the annual updates around the holidays grew shorter and shorter until they disappeared altogether.

And now I've nothing. I'm alone. Few people remember

---

15 For a different view of the relationship, see Mary Osborne's roman á clef, *Beauty and the Beast, 2.0* (Netflix Books, 2038). The documentary film *Mary Quite Contrary* covers the subsequent he-said, she-said controversy.

my name. I'm sick, so very sick. And yet there I was—or, at least, there my avatar was—walking with my ex-wife in what seemed like a veritable Garden of Eden. Except that I couldn't smell its roses or taste its fruits.

Rachel showed me the medical clinic with the herb garden in back, where a midwife was applying a poultice to the forehead of a patient. She showed me the one-room schoolhouse—with a library of real books culled from basements throughout the area—where the students were rehearsing *A Midsummer Night's Dream*. She showed me the distillery—in a section of the barn containing large vats and a maze of piping—where the community produced its own orange liqueur. She showed me her own tidy room in the dormer of the common house, with its narrow bed, African violets on the windowsill, and framed prints from old botany textbooks on the wall. She introduced me to some of the other commune members: not the monkish types with long scraggly beards and poorly patched sweaters I'd expected, but a group who could have been Rachel's colleagues at some university. Indeed, they were generally politer and better behaved than academics, albeit with more calluses on their hands.

As we were leaving the common house, I glimpsed something on the wall and stopped. It was a sign that read: "Gun Room."

"Is this left over from when this was a working farm?" I asked.

"No," Rachel said. She pulled a keychain from her pocket, unlocked the door, and ushered me inside. "I might as well show you, even though it's not yet been VR-secured. You're the first avatar we've had here in ten years."

"I appreciate the exception you've made for—" I began, then stopped.

In locked cabinets that ringed the room was every kind of gun, from old-fashioned assault rifles to the latest in nanoweaponry. I must have been standing with my mouth open, because Rachel had to wave her hand in front of my face to get my attention.

"It's just a good idea to be prepared," she said.

"Prepared for what? You've got enough firepower here to fight World War III!"

"Not really," she replied, guiding me out of the room. "But it is enough to defend Arcadia. All of our children receive training in marksmanship. Even I've become a good shot. We do a fair amount of hunting too, to keep down the deer population and stock the larder."

"Have you been attacked?"

"Not in some time."

"But you have reason to believe that—"

"I certainly don't have to explain to you, Julian, the direction the world is heading. This is a comfortable setup. You can imagine how the White Tigers or a splinter of the Caliphate might like to set up shop here. You're an avatar, so we vetted you virtually. You didn't see the actual security perimeter. Not exactly a castle with a moat, but pretty close."

"I just thought that—"

"That what? We were a peace commune? Well, we are. But we're also not a stupid commune. The stupid ones have already been invaded and occupied. Outside these walls, you take your life into your hands. And there are a lot of wolves out there that we mustn't inadvertently let through our gates."[16]

"Wide is the gate," I mumbled.

"Exactly. Even one mistake could be fatal. Like a single pathogen in a healthy body."

"Listen, Rachel, there's something I want to tell you. Can we go somewhere private?"

She hesitated, then said, "Let's go back to my room."

We sat on her bed. I marveled at how sun-filled and comfortable the small space was. I imagined that it smelled of oatmeal soap and dried rose petals. I had a sudden memory of sitting on Rachel's bed in Cambridge when she was a graduate student and we'd just met. She was telling me about ice and I thought that I'd never met anyone who could speak with such passion on a topic I'd hitherto found so numbingly boring. And here we were again, not so much circling back but spiraling around to meet up again at different points in our lives.

"Is it about one of our children?" Rachel asked.

---

16 The security environment in northern Vermont had deteriorated around this time, owing to the attacks the Quebecois government launched against the White Tiger units operating on its territory. Forced across the border into Vermont, those units established camps from which they had mounted several attacks on communes like Arcadia.

"No, it's about me. You can't tell from my avatar, but I'm very sick."

"How sick?"

"A couple weeks, maybe a couple days."

"I see." She reached out her hand, but there was nothing to hold onto. "I'm sorry, Julian."

"However, there's this treatment . . ."

"Do you need money? I'm sure that Gordon would—"

"No, not money. This trip around the world has been to prepare a report, a kind of update of *Splinterlands*—in exchange for the treatment."

"The sales of the book will cover the treatment?"

"No, that's not it. A corporation was interested in my research. My perspective. So we worked out a deal."

"What kind of treatment?"

"Something very experimental, but the early results are amazing."

"I'm glad to hear that, Julian."

"I negotiated not one but two courses of treatment as part of the deal. For two people."

"You want to know if there's someone here who's sick? What is it, cancer?"

"More like a new infection that's spreading rather quickly. In me. But also out there in the world.[17] But that's not what I'm talking about. I'm talking about you."

"But I'm not sick."

---

17 The PNC3 staph infection that West had caught would eventually kill 1.3 million people worldwide.

"They've developed a kind of regeneration therapy that won't just cure my illness. It will extend my life. I don't know for how long. Possibly as much as two decades. At which point, some other therapy might be available and—"

"Julian, really? You want to live forever?"

"I'm not ready to die. Not yet anyway. And if you take the treatment too—"

"What kind of treatment is it?"

"Gene therapy. The immune system. I don't really know how it works."

"CRISPR."

"Yes, CRISPR."

"Clustered, regularly interspaced short palindromic repeats," Rachel said.

"Uh, that sounds about right."

"You negotiated a deal with CRISPR International."[18]

"Yes. They contacted me a year ago. They were very interested in my work and . . ."

"Why would CRISPR International be interested in your work? They're a biotech company."

"They said that they commission reports all the time to help them understand the world better."

"To help them make more money."

"I suppose, but this treatment could transform humanity. It could take us to another level of evolution."

---

18 Other corporations had used the CRISPR technology, but CRISPR International had effectively bought out its competitors. It subsequently protected its monopoly with an arsenal of patents and lawyers.

"All of us? Or some of us?"

"S—Some of us," I stuttered, then recovered. "Just like Arcadia is not for all of us, just some of us."

"I've heard things about CRISPR International. But perhaps they're the same things you've heard."[19]

"As soon as I deliver my report, I'll start the treatment. And you can, too, Rachel."

"And then what's your plan? I should come and live with you wherever you are these days?"

"No," I said. "I made a mistake all those years ago."[20]

---

[19] By that time, a number of exposés of CRISPR International had revealed the corporation's record of bribery, falsified trial results, and financial misconduct. See, for example, the report *Whispers about CRISPR* (Institute for Policy Studies, 2048).

[20] West could be referring to any number of mistakes, from his decision not to follow Rachel to Arcadia to his concealment of his other family. Of course, the two were related. In May 2021, Rachel Leopold took her husband on a surprise cruise to Nova Scotia to celebrate the success of *Splinterlands*. In what I've determined to be nothing more than a coincidence, Alesha Kinbote was working on board as a hostess. If it hadn't been for the worldwide success of his book, Alesha might not have recognized her first husband, since they hadn't seen each other in more than thirty years. But thanks to the author photo, widely reproduced elsewhere, she did, and she confronted West that first night when he and Rachel appeared for dinner. West tried to pull Rachel away from her, suggesting that they eat at one of the other restaurants on the ship, but when Alesha began crying and murmuring, "Isaac, poor Isaac," Rachel refused. Although West successfully avoided Alesha for the remainder of the cruise, Rachel was relentless in getting information out of her husband. She even managed one painful conversation with Alesha herself. After that, of course, everything changed. West continued to take considerable pains to conceal the full story, particularly as it related to the notorious kidnapping in Antioquia. What he did divulge, however, was enough to damage

"That means you want to come here?"

"If you'll have me."

"It's not my decision, Julian. We decide by consensus."

"But you'll think about it?"

She gazed at me searchingly. She turned her head to look out the window at the purple and orange glow of the sunset. Then she turned back to me and smiled.

"Julian," she said.

And then she vanished.

---

his marriage irreparably and provoke Gordon and Aurora into severing relations with him.

CHAPTER 6

In Extremis

I was back in my bed. The VR apparatus was gone. Ivanov and Gletkin were standing over me.

"Where is he?" Gletkin asked in his tinny voice.

"I was just with my ex-wife, with Rachel," I replied, dazed by my sudden extraction. It felt as if I'd been woken from a dream. "I was in Vermont. In Arcadia. She was going to tell me whether she would take the treatment with me. It's really important that I go back there and . . ."

"Your son, Benjamin," Ivanov clarified. "Where is he?"

The two men worked for CRISPR International. I knew that much. They'd gotten in touch with me a year ago with their proposal. Ivanov and Gletkin were not their real names. I've forgotten those. As always, they were dressed like those FBI agents I contacted so many years ago—black suits, white shirts, black ties, grey fedoras—so I thought of them as agents as well. Agents of my salvation, perhaps. They were not Russian, for they seemed to be native speakers of English. I'd given them the names of characters from one of my favorite novels—Ivanov the good cop and Gletkin the bad.[1]

Gletkin was small, very thin, almost like a teenage boy, but with an outsized head that lacked all facial hair except for two pale dashes for eyebrows. His large eyes and long fingers gave him more than a passing resemblance to a lemur. Ivanov, on the other hand, was immense, almost as broad as he was tall, like a huge side of beef. I came to think of Gletkin as feral and Ivanov as drowsy and domesticated. Over their black-and-white uniforms, what I couldn't see but knew must be there was the transparent bio-gear that protected them from my infection.

"My son Benjamin?" I asked, confused and trying to sort out my thoughts. "That was yesterday, when I visited him."

"We know when you visited him," Gletkin said, rubbing his bald head as if polishing a white eggplant. "You were at the Hotel President. And then you walked out with him. You got into a hovercar. You drove to Francistown. It took you three hours and fourteen minutes. You didn't choose the most direct route either. And you took a detour to stop in Serowe. But neither of you stepped out of the car when it landed."

"You seem to know a lot about my trip to Botswana."

"You drove to Francistown," Ivanov continued, his plump fingers tented in front of him. "When you got there, you

---

1 The book is Arthur Koestler's *Darkness at Noon* (1940), but it's not clear why West decided to borrow these particular character names.

stopped at the central market and you both got out of the car. And it turned out that it wasn't you. And it wasn't Benjamin either."

I had no idea what they were talking about. I kept quiet.

"Who hijacked your apparatus?" Gletkin practically shouted at me. He was pacing briskly back and forth by my bed in a fit of impatience, like a little boy who had to go to the bathroom. "We have the best of the best, an absolutely world-class tech team. We need to know who these hackers are. We need to shut down their operation and turn their coders. This is a matter of the highest urgency."

"Can you help us with any additional information, Doctor West?" Ivanov asked me politely.

"I was at the Hotel President," I said carefully. "I met my son there. We talked for a few minutes. And then he, well, he dismissed me."

"I saw the readout." Gletkin continued to pace. "We had full-spectrum coverage. And he still disappeared. All we need is one more data point to start tracking him down. Can you give us this one data point?"

"He didn't tell me anything."

"This is very important," Ivanov said softly. "Is there any information you can give us?"

"He's no longer fighting the Caliphate."

Gletkin drew uncomfortably close to me. His retinal implants had rendered his irises completely black, giving him even more of the look of a lemur. "I've scanned the Interpol briefings. I know that he's not fighting the Caliphate. That's not new information for us. You're giving us old information. I should tell you: I am authorized to use nonlethal interrogation techniques."

Ivanov put a hand on his colleague's shoulder. "There's no need for that."

"He said he's involved in something new," I blurted out. "Dealing with a new threat."

"You're supposed to be doing research for us," Gletkin said, tilting his head as if he were conducting an infosearch. "This is not research. This is not what we're paying for."

Ivanov squeezed his colleague's shoulder to get his attention. "Let's see if they've had any luck retrieving the tracking feed."

"Tracking feed?" I asked. "Tracking what?"

"Tracking you." Gletkin dismissed me with a hand gesture. "And listening to your conversations. I am not the best judge of the art of conversation, but it seems to me that they were very boring."

I turned to Ivanov. "You were watching? And recording?"

Gletkin had gone back to rubbing is skull. "These mercenaries are professionals. The tracking feed has been wiped clean. We must rely on HUMINT."

Ivanov waggled his plump fingers in my direction. "Take a little rest. We'll be back in a few minutes."

They left the room.

I had risen on my elbows to talk to them. Now I collapsed on my pillow. I was so frustrated that I could cry. I had been so near to securing Rachel's agreement. All I needed was the VR apparatus. One more visit would do the trick. Then, with Rachel on board, I would dictate my update to *Splinterlands* and start the treatment. We would both start it, and I could finally leave this place.

I'd already spent a month in this white room in the CRISPR International headquarters in the Northern Territories, on a hill above the capital city. They'd flown me here on their corporate jet when I first showed signs of infection, and the medical staff immediately started me on a course of drugs to slow the disease that was eating through me like a wild animal.[2] For the last month I had been hooked up wirelessly to monitors and by tubes to any number of life-sustaining drips, doing research for my report during the day and watching an endless stream of movies from my youth at night. Ivanov and Gletkin had gone over my itinerary with me endlessly, asking me what I hoped to learn from my conversations with my children, from my reunion with my ex-wife. Only when my condition had more or less stabilized did they let me embark on the trip. What none of us knew was how long the window would remain open. Without the therapy, it was simple enough: I would die. With it, I had a shot at living forever.

I should have anticipated surveillance—and they should have told me. I would have welcomed it. My memory isn't

---

2 CRISPR tracked West down to a pod hotel in a rundown neighborhood in Toronto. He had already contracted the PNC3 staph infection when "Ivanov" and "Gletkin" first contacted him. The symptoms only began to manifest later, of course.

as good as it once was. It would be useful to have a visual transcript of my travels as I prepare my report. But there were things that the two agents said that I didn't understand. Little wonder, since I was so woozy from my exertions and the VR equivalent of jetlag. Still, why were they so interested in Benjamin's whereabouts?

I was tired. I wanted to take a short nap. Then I would begin my report. Once I provided my report, I was sure that they would let me return to Arcadia, to Rachel. They would make good on their side of the bargain.

Some people in my condition might want to live longer simply to see if the world pulls through its present, seemingly terminal crisis. That's not me. I'm aware of the more optimistic analyses out there. Not long ago, someone forwarded me an extraordinarily popular TED talk on the "coming consensus" in which a telegenic pundit argued that, even though we are now at a nadir of cooperation, some new form of centralization and globalization must lie just beyond the horizon.[3] It's not a completely farfetched notion. Dreams of global cooperation are everywhere. Even the jihadis operating their micro-Caliphates around the world aspire to unite the faithful under a single banner, while fundamentalists of so many other religions and political faiths similarly look forward to their day of eschatological victory. Incredibly, there are still diplomats who hope to get all 400-plus members of the United Nations to agree to the sorts of institutional

---

3 I have not been able to identify this TED talk. West might be misremembering.

reforms that could provide the world with some semblance of global governance. And maybe a green swan *is* swimming out there somewhere, some new killer app that will put every single person on the same page, literally.

As a geo-paleontologist, I'm reluctant to speculate about such schemes. Anyone can make predictions, but none of these scenarios of future integration seems plausible to me. "That's the way the cookie crumbles," we used to say when I was a kid. And a cookie can only crumble in one direction.

Still, as long as I am with Rachel, I would be content to watch the cookie crumble from the safety and comfort of Arcadia. And perhaps it really isn't too late. As long as we have breath in our chests, humans can't help but hope.

Only today can we all see clearly, as I wrote so many years ago, that the rise of the splinterlands has been humanity's true tragedy. This is what I've learned in my research, in my "travels." The inability of cultures to compromise within single states anticipated our current era, when multiplying nation-states can't compromise on a single planet to address our global scourges. The glue that once held us together—namely, solidarity across religion, ethnicity, and class—has lost its binding force. We somehow lost the ability to intuit the common humanity that bound us together regardless of our obvious differences. But perhaps we can create those bonds again, family by family, commune by commune—not on arid Mars but in the few green pockets left on Earth . . .

I might have dozed off, because suddenly they were back in the room. They didn't look happy.

"They're not talking," Gletkin was saying, cradling his skull as if it were a fragile egg. "We have no leads. We're basically back to zero. Zero. I want to initiate the nonlethal interrogation protocol."

"Denied." Ivanov turned to me and spoke in a reassuring voice. "We need to find out where your son Benjamin is. It's very important."

"Perhaps after I've filed my report, I can go back to Botswana—"

Gletkin placed his hands over his ears and winced in imaginary pain. "I don't want to hear about the report. The very mention of the report causes my system to crash. You don't get it, do you? We know everything about you. Everything. All your little secrets.[4] But there's one thing we do not know, only one, and that's the most important thing in the world."

"Right now, the whereabouts of your son are more important than the report," Ivanov said.

"Why are you so interested in my son?"

"The problem," Gletkin replied, raising his voice, "is that your son is interested in us."

Ivanov seemed upset by his colleague's comment. He cleared his throat.

"Your son," Gletkin continued in a more contained

---

4 In 2052, WikiLeaks published several internal memos from CRISPR International concerning the Julian West case. They revealed that the organization knew every detail about the Isaac Kinbote affair, including the circumstances of his death. CRISPR already had a well-established track record of using blackmail to secure the support of influential politicians and respected scientists.

tone, "is not interested in progress. He wants to stop the trials of the regeneration treatment, the same treatment we'll be giving you if you deliver as promised."

"Why would he want to do that?"

Ivanov opened his mouth to speak, paused, and then began again. "You understand, of course, that the treatment will only be available to a limited number of people. There are simply too many people on the planet right now. If we extended everyone's lifespan, we would run out of food and water fast."

"But that's already the case," I pointed out. "And the temperature is continuing to rise."

"Thank God," Gletkin exclaimed with no emotion. "The Earth is doing what comes naturally. What did your John Muir say? 'Earth hath no sorrows that Earth cannot heal.' It's shedding excess weight. It's on a diet so that it can be a smaller planet. Even I can see that this is a good thing."

"We need to find your son," Ivanov continued. "We think he has in his possession—"

"He stole it from our Botswana trials, the . . ."

Ivanov silenced his colleague with the barest movement of his index finger. "We think that he has a sample of the treatment and the means of reproducing it. On a massive scale."

I suddenly realized the problem. "He'll give it away for free. Like Robin Hood."[5]

---

5 West drew his conclusion from the information the CRISPR agents supplied. It's not at all clear, however, that Benjamin ever intended to univer-

"He might as well be giving out cyanide pills." Gletkin resumed his pacing. "If everyone lives forever, no one lives forever. It doesn't require a supercomputer. Even you can do the math."

"So, you understand, we need to stop him," Ivanov added.

"Well . . ." I paused. I was trying to work something out. Gletkin stopped in his tracks. "Well, what?"

"Well . . ." My voice trailed off.

"Even your other children understand the importance of stopping him!" Gletkin shouted at me.

I glanced back and forth between the agents. I was trying to integrate this new information. "What do you mean, my other children understand?" I asked. "How do you know?"

"What's important—" Ivanov began.

But his partner cut him short and again got close to my face. "You think this is a charity? You think we fly every old dinosaur out here to save his worthless life?"

"How do you know what my children think?" I said again, slowly.

"We simply asked them a few questions," Ivanov replied. "And they were very cooperative."

"You kidnapped them," I said.

"Of course we did!" Gletkin blurted out. His black eyes seemed to spark as if he were suffering from an electric shock or a seizure.

---

salize the treatment. In light of his subsequent conduct, it was clear that he wanted to force CRISPR to make other treatments available at cost to vulnerable populations and break the company's monopoly.

"I'll do whatever you want," I said. My pulse was racing, and one of the monitors began to emit an insistent set of beeps. "As long as you release them."[6]

Ivanov eyed the monitor nervously. "Calm down. We didn't kidnap them. We simply invited them to an all-expenses-paid information-sharing session. Eventually we'll fly them home again."

"They don't know anything," I pleaded. "Please let them go—I'll do anything, just please—"

"We need you to do only one thing," Ivanov replied in a soothing voice.

All the pieces were now falling into place, and I thought I might finally be seeing the full picture. "This whole deal. This trip. You don't care about my report. You were just using me as bait. To get whatever you wanted from my children. To find Benjamin."

"We're genuinely committed to your report," Ivanov reassured me.[7]

---

6 This exchange must have elicited a feeling of déjà vu in West. Isaac Kinbote, too, had been kidnapped—in Antioquia, after his cover as a drug smuggler was blown. CARSI followed protocol and refused to acknowledge that he was its agent. The cartel that Kinbote had infiltrated managed to turn up his link to Alesha and, through her, to Julian West. It quietly made an offer to West: the life of his son in exchange for a positive profile of the cartel's leader in a major publication. This was in January 2021, after *Splinterlands* hit number four on the *New York Times* nonfiction bestseller list.

7 One of the leaked CRISPR memos discusses West's psychology and whether he would respond more positively to carrots or sticks. "West is ultimately most concerned about his reputation," the memo read. "So, it will be important to offer him a sufficiently large carrot to engage his participation,

"You waited to see if I got the information you needed. When I didn't, you grabbed Aurora and Gordon and brought them here. Or wherever. You had no right! We made a deal. I would prepare the report . . ."

"Forget the report," Gletkin said. "If you don't give us what we want, we'll pull out all your tubes, one by one. I want to hear what those monitors sound like together. I'm guessing a symphony."

Ivanov fixed his colleague with a withering stare. "You obviously need an attitude adjustment.[8] I want you to report to IT after this."

He shrugged. The sparks faded from his eyes. "You're the boss."

"I told you: I don't know where Benjamin is," I said.

"We know that your youngest son would like to see his mother again," Ivanov said. "That's the only thing that would draw him into the open."

"So, you're going to kidnap my ex-wife?"

"You saw the gun room," Gletkin interjected. "No one gets in without their say-so."

"And we're not exactly welcome guests at Arcadia," Ivanov pointed out. "But *you* are."

"We're making sure right now that the people your terrorist son runs with know that Rachel is dying."

"He will soon be on his way to Arcadia."

---

and this carrot should be connected in some way to his book *Splinterlands*."
8 "Ivanov" was referring to the TAAT, or Turing Attitude Adjustment Test, a well-known diagnostic tool that West obviously had never heard of.

"And so will we, thanks to you," Gletkin concluded.

"Why do you even need me anymore?" I asked, feeling short of breath. "You can just steal my avatar and send it there without me."

"True," Ivanov said. "But we don't want to arouse suspicions. Your son and his colleagues use very sophisticated software. We want you on board, Doctor West. We want you to help us save the world. This is a second chance for you and for humanity."

"We'll tell you exactly what to say and what to do," Gletkin said. "And we'll monitor you to make sure you follow the script precisely."

Ivanov rested his hands on the side of my bed. I found his immensity menacing now, not reassuring. "This is a vital assignment."

"You have exactly one hour," Gletkin said. "To make the right decision."

"We're counting on you," Ivanov added with a smile.

I watched them leave. My decision was so obvious I didn't even need to think about it.

At the beginning of the Great Unraveling, I naively believed that we all lived in a common home. Some rooms were in terrible disrepair. Those sheltering in the attic were often exposed to the elements. The house as a whole needed better insulation, more efficient appliances, and solar panels on the roof, and we had indeed fallen behind on the mortgage payments. But like so many of my peers, I seldom doubted that we could scrape together the funds and the will to make the necessary repairs by asking the richer residents of the house to pay their fair share. Surely we would all pull together.

Thirty-five years and endless catastrophes later, on a poorer, bleaker, less hospitable planet, it's clear that we just weren't paying sufficient attention. Had we been listening, we would have heard the termites. There, in the basement of our common home, they were eating the very foundations out from under us.

Suddenly, before we knew what was happening, all that was solid had melted into air.

I have now sent out a version of this report, without all the personal information, as the attachment to my note to Rachel. Ivanov and Gletkin saw no harm in that. They don't really care about it anyway. They read through it only to make sure that I hadn't given away any secrets or included any contrary messages. Perhaps someday, somewhere, somehow this full version will be published in some form. Perhaps it will be read by some people. But like everything I've ever done in my life, it comes too late to have any real impact beyond personal aggrandizement, and even that no longer matters.

I wrote Rachel to expect me—to expect my avatar—in two days, when I would renew my offer. She responded immediately that she was looking forward to seeing me again, without further comment about the offer. I don't think she ever would have really entertained such a thing. Organic food and gene-replacement therapy just don't go hand in hand. In exchange for my cooperation, the two agents gave me the time to finish this full and final report. And they showed me what I most wanted to see: live feeds of Aurora and Gordon returning home to their families.[9]

They gave me, in other words, a second chance. This time I won't blow it.[10]

I took my remaining time, the time I told them I needed to memorize my script for the visit to Arcadia, to finish this full report. I have set it up to go to both Aurora and Gordon in one month's time, when I trust that the two agents will no longer be on my case.[11]

The tubes are lying on the floor. Gletkin was right. The sounds of all the monitors beeping together do resem-

---

9 Both Aurora and Gordon are still alive. Aurora is reportedly preparing the second volume of her memoir. Gordon has established a Kinbote Fellowship at Xinjiang Technical University. Benjamin continues to operate clandestinely.

10 It might be useful at this point to quote from a document available at the Kinbote Memorial Center, whose executive director I was from 2053 to 2058. "There is no evidence that Isaac Kinbote ever revealed his true identity to his kidnappers," the document read. "West offered money. But the cartel was not interested in money, of which it had plenty. It wanted legitimacy and the backing of more powerful outside interests, which the cartel could use to challenge and then capture the Antioquian state." West worried that such a profile would expose his connection to Isaac Kinbote. He believed at that time, a full year before the Nova Scotia cruise, that he could keep his secret indefinitely. In her memoir, Aurora discusses the way her father wrestled with the dilemma for some time before ultimately deciding not to respond to the cartel's final ultimatum. West might also have believed that the cartel was bluffing. It wasn't.

11 This document is West's full report, with all the personal information restored. I have corrected the obvious typographical mistakes and added these explanatory footnotes. A companion volume, which consists of Rachel Leopold's memoir plus annotations, is currently being prepared for publication.

ble a symphony, something minimalist and repetitive, like a work by Philip Glass. With the last of my energy, I've pushed the hospital bed up against the door. In other words, I've made my bed, and now I am lying in it.

By the time they manage to push the door open, it will be too late. So much for immortality.

"Wide is the gate through which I will come to see you, dear Rachel," I wrote at the end of the letter to my ex-wife. She'll know exactly what I mean and will act accordingly.

Outside, the world is experiencing the fire next time. But in here, I feel a chill. I no longer see the embers. My story is over.

And soon I, too, will melt into air.

Acknowledgements

This book would not be possible without Tom Engelhardt, who encouraged me to write the initial essay for *TomDispatch* and then, at the suggestion of Nick Turse, urged me to turn it into this short novel. Tom has been an expert editor and has contributed much to providing the polish to this project. I'd also like to thank Nick and Karin Lee for reading earlier drafts and providing excellent suggestions, and Sarah Grey for careful copyediting. Finally, I'd like to thank my colleagues John Cavanagh, Ethelbert Miller, Jim Lobe, Peter Certo, Jasmin Ramsey, and the rest of the crew at the Institute for Policy Studies for creating a work environment that allows for creative enterprises and, as importantly, for working daily to prevent such dystopian scenarios from becoming a reality.

About the Author

John Feffer is a playwright and the author of several books including the novel *Foamers*. His articles have appeared in the *New York Times*, the *Washington Post*, the *Nation*, *Salon*, and others. He is the director of Foreign Policy In Focus at the Institute for Policy Studies.